CHAPTER 1 – THE WATCHERS IN THE VAN

The van smelled like cold coffee, cheap sugar, and men who'd been sitting too long with nowhere to go.

Agent Knight shouldered the door closed with his back, clutching two steaming Styrofoam cups and a flimsy white box dotted with grease. The late-night Houston air was already fading off his jacket by the time he squeezed down the cramped aisle.

"Anything happen while I was gone?" he asked.

Agent Barber didn't answer right away. His eyes were glued to the wall of monitors stacked in front of him—a glowing grid of surveillance angles on the King estate across the street. Driveway. Front gate. Side yard. DJ King's office lit in soft amber.

"Yeah," Barber finally said. "He took a run at the maid for about forty-five minutes."

Knight grimaced as he handed over a coffee. "Jesus. I was gone twenty minutes."

"Time moves different when you're rich." Barber smirked, flipping open the donut box and plucking out a glazed ring. "Now he's back in his study drinking cognac and smoking a cigar."

Knight leaned toward the largest monitor. DJ King sat behind a heavy desk, haloed in low lamp light, smoke curling around his head like a crown. From a distance he looked more like a retired senator than a crime boss—perfect suit, expensive watch, nothing out of place.

"Can you believe it?" Knight muttered. "We're stuck in this smelly van while he sits in his castle getting his dick pulled by some babe, smoking cigars."

"She was doing way more than that," Barber said casually.

Knight gagged. "Aww, c'mon."

Barber just laughed and licked sugar from his fingers.

On the monitors, the maid slipped out of the office adjusting her hair. DJ King barely glanced up. He took another slow pull from his cigar and stared at the door long after it closed, expression unreadable.

Barber adjusted a dial. A thin green bar slid across a different monitor, tracking audio feed. "We need him relaxed," he said. "Let him enjoy his life. Happy bosses talk more."

Knight bit into a donut and chased it with too-hot coffee. Outside, Houston was unusually quiet—no sirens, no shouting, just the distant whoosh of cars on wet asphalt.

Then a soft electronic chime cut through the van.

Both men froze.

Barber glanced at the audio board. One of the

TABLE OF CONTENTS

The King Empire: Book One

Chapter 1 – The Watchers in the Van
Chapter 2 – Cream at Club Split
Chapter 3 – Streets, Smoke, and Blood
Chapter 4 – Cream at Club Split
Chapter 5 – Roxy's Job
Chapter 6 – Calls, Champagne, and a Setup
Chapter 7 – Basement Baptism
Chapter 8 – The Council of Wolves
Chapter 9 – Sniper on the Roof
Chapter 10 – The FBI Briefing
Chapter 11 – Family Business
Chapter 12 – Turk's Warehouse Massacre
Chapter 13 – Funeral Home Logistics
Chapter 14 – Massage Parlor Conspiracy
Chapter 15 – LJ and Michelle
Chapter 16 – Jasmine vs. Ha Jung
Chapter 17 – Javier's Fear
Chapter 18 – The Stripper Assassins
Chapter 19 – The Parlor Trap
Chapter 20 – DJ, Mac, and the Nephew
Chapter 21 – The Flores Cartel Falls
Chapter 22 – The Empire Shifts
Chapter 23 – Harvey Walks In

Chapter 24 – Harvey's Collapse
Chapter 25 – James Sees the Cracks
Chapter 26 – Loyalty & Lies
Chapter 27 – A King's Son

Chapter 28 – Before the Fall *(Final Chapter)*

channels was lighting up—DJ King's secure landline.

"Shh," he whispered. "Incoming call."

Static hissed, then snapped into focus as Barber twisted the volume knob.

A man's voice came through—smooth, tight, carrying weight.

"We have a problem on our hands, Mr. King."

Knight stiffened. "That's Harris," he whispered. "The lawyer."

DJ's voice replied from another speaker, calm as still water.

"What's going on, Harris? Everything alright with Tammy and my grandbaby?"

Barber darted his gaze between the waveforms and the live feed of DJ in his office, the crime boss leaning back in his chair with the receiver to his ear.

"Yeah, everyone's fine," Harris said quickly. "This is… something else."

DJ's brow dipped. "Well spit it out."

A pause. You could almost hear Harris deciding how to phrase it.

"One of your accounts has been compromised."

Knight and Barber exchanged a look. *Compromised* was not a word anyone wanted associated with the Kings.

On-screen, DJ King went motionless. Then he slowly

leaned forward, cigar hovering over the ashtray.

"How much is missing?"

Knight grabbed a notepad reflexively, even though the software was recording every word.

"One hundred and fifty million," Harris said.

The number detonated in the van.

Knight let out a low whistle. Barber didn't move.

"One-fifty?" Knight mouthed.

"Somebody either real brave," Barber said quietly, "or real stupid."

On the monitor, DJ gently set the cigar down like he was placing a chess piece.

"Come to the house first thing in the morning," he said. "I don't trust these lines. We'll talk then."

"You want your nephew in attendance?" Harris asked.

Knight underlined *nephew* three times.

DJ's eyes flicked up—straight toward one of his own surveillance cameras.

"No," he said. "Leave him out of this."

Barber circled the word *him* twice.

Harris lowered his voice. "Is the van still parked outside the gate?"

Both agents froze.

On-screen, DJ inhaled from his cigar and stared

directly into the camera feed, as if he were looking straight through the monitors into their eyes.

"Yeah," DJ said. "It's still there."

Harris exhaled hard. "Fucking Feds. Alright. See you in the morning."

The line clicked dead.

Silence swallowed the van.

"Shit," Barber breathed.

Knight forced air into his lungs. "Who the hell would be dumb enough to steal from DJ King?"

"Someone with a death wish."

Knight reached for the keys dangling from the dash. "Let's get back to HQ. Ware needs to—"

Headlights flared across the monitors.

Barber leaned closer and flipped to the gate feed. A black sedan rolled to a stop. The security camera caught the driver's face as he leaned toward the callbox.

Barber grabbed his binoculars.

"Oh, you gotta be kidding me," he said. "That is the one and only Lue King. DJ's little brother."

Knight sank back. "Guess we're not going anywhere."

The gate slid open, swallowing the sedan.

Barber settled into his seat, brushing crumbs off his shirt. "Yeah. Looks that way."

Outside, the King estate glowed warm and unbothered in the Houston night.

Inside the van, the agents had no idea that before sunrise, bodies would be scattered across the city...
a sniper would make history...
and the name **LJ King** would become the most expensive name in Houston.

CHAPTER 2 – CREAM AT CLUB SPLIT

Houston's night pulsed neon on the other side of the city.

Club Split's line wrapped around the block—women in glitter heels hugging themselves against the chill, men checking watches and sizing each other up. Bass thumped through the walls, a low heartbeat promising everything and nothing.

Marco Flores pulled up to the curb in a sleek black car, engine purring like it respected him. He stepped out slow, dressed sharp enough to cut the air—tailored jacket, fresh fade, a hint of chain at his throat.

The valet hustled over. Marco dropped the keys into his hand without breaking stride.

"Scratch it," he said in Spanish, "and I'll scratch you."

The valet laughed nervously. Marco did not.

Inside, the hallway to Jasmine King's office smelled like perfume, spilled liquor, and ambition. The bass softened to a distant thud, replaced by the clink of glassware and VIP murmurs.

Jasmine sat behind her desk, legs crossed, black dress fitting her like confidence. Her twin brother James leaned against the bar nearby, glasses catching the light.

"Think he'll go for it?" James asked.

"If he's smart," Jasmine said.

"He wasn't the sharpest in school."

She glanced at him. "People grow."

"Some people," James said. "But I still think we should hit the others first."

Jasmine rose just as the door opened.

Marco walked in like he owned the oxygen. "Why am I here?" he asked. "Shouldn't you be talking to my brother?"

James pushed off the bar and poured two shots. "I agree with you. We should be."

"But," Jasmine said with a razor smile, "I told my brother I wanted to talk to *you* first."

Marco eyed the drink, then her, then sat and tossed it back.

"Alright," he said. "Talk."

Jasmine clasped her hands. "Me and my brother are expanding. We want to buy your clubs."

Marco's brows lifted. "This your father talking?"

James bristled, but Jasmine stayed calm. "My father has no stake in this. This deal stays in this room."

James slid onto the armrest of a chair, spinning the empty glass between his fingers.

"We're willing," he said, "to pay you three times what your clubs are worth."

Marco whistled. "Three times. Damn. Y'all must really love nightclubs."

"Not really," James said. "We just love money."

He reached into his pocket and pulled out a tiny glass vial filled with off-white powder—innocent as sugar.

"And this," he said, "is about to make us a fuck ton of it."

He tossed it to Marco, who caught it easily.

"What's this?" Marco asked.

"The future," Jasmine said.

Marco cracked it open. Another drug, another Tuesday—until he poured a line across the back of his hand and sniffed.

The effect hit instantly.

His pupils blew wide. Energy tightened and loosened through him all at once. The room sharpened. Music from the floor below snapped into clarity. His skin buzzed, but his mind felt clean.

"Oh shit," he breathed. "It's not coke."

"No," James said, pleased. "It's called Cream. Hits ten times harder than molly—"

"Without the side effects," Jasmine added. "So. Do we have a deal?"

Marco laughed at nothing, marveling at the sensation in his fingers. Then the high steadied enough for his thinking to catch up.

"I'd gladly sell for three times," he said. "If I could."

Jasmine's smile thinned.

"But my father won't go for it," Marco continued. "The clubs wash too much of his money."

James leaned forward. "You can open ten more clubs with what we're offering."

"True," Marco said. "But why fix something that ain't broke?"

He met Jasmine's gaze directly now—and something in her eyes made his heart thump harder. Something calculating. Something final.

Jasmine folded her hands. Professional. Polite.

"Well," she said. "Thank you for your time. Enjoy the club tonight."

Marco stood, still feeling the Cream humming beneath his skin. "I think I will. And I'm keeping this."

He pocketed the vial and left laughing.

The moment the door clicked shut, James turned to his sister. "What now?"

Jasmine finished her drink. Set the glass down.

"Get me Roxy."

As if summoned, her secretary peeked in. "Miss

King? Your guests arrived in VIP."

Jasmine smiled. "Coming."

When the door closed again, she looked down through the office window. Lights strobed. Bodies moved. Money flowed like water.

Marco Flores thought the conversation ended.

Jasmine King knew better.

In her world, **no** was just the moment you decided *how somebody was going to die*.

CHAPTER 3 – STREETS, SMOKE, AND BLOOD

Dawn came slow over Houston, a pale smear of light stretching across the low clouds. The city wasn't awake yet—too early for traffic, too late for drunks. Just that strange dead zone where only criminals, bakers, and the unlucky moved.

Tony Lucio stood outside his coffee shop on Westheimer, a steaming espresso in one hand, a cigarette in the other. The old man wore a wool coat despite the humidity, silver hair slicked back, the heavy creases in his face carved by years of bad decisions and good profits.

Next to him, Joey Fingers paced the sidewalk like his shoes were on fire.

"Richie shoulda been home last night," Joey snapped. "My kid don't disappear. Not without calling. Not without something happening."

Tony blew a lazy ribbon of smoke at the rising sun. "Relax, Joey. He's probably laid up with some girl, sleeping off whatever bullshit he got into."

"This ain't like him." Joey jabbed a finger at the ground. "He's been running pickups for those Dominican kids. I told him stay away. I told him—"

Tony waved the cigarette. "Yeah, yeah, you told him. Kids don't listen. They gotta learn 'no' the hard way."

Joey paced faster, hands flapping the way that earned him his nickname. "I'm telling you, Tone, something's wrong. I can feel it. I know my boy."

Tony lowered his espresso and looked at him with something close to sympathy.

"You wanna send some men sniffing around? Fine. Do it. But don't panic until you got a body."

Joey swallowed. Hard.

A gust of morning breeze rolled down the empty street, carrying the smell of wet asphalt and fresh bread from the kitchen behind them. A delivery truck murmured in the distance. One of Tony's younger soldiers—Vinny—leaned on the brick wall nearby, scrolling his phone. Two others finished sweeping the sidewalk.

Quiet. Too quiet.

Tony flicked his cigarette into the gutter. "Let's get inside. I got a meeting with the unions at eight—"

He stopped.

Not because of a sound, but because of the absence of one.

For a split second, the street felt hollow. Like it was holding its breath.

Then the motorcycle came.

A matte-black sport bike shot around the corner, engine screaming like a banshee. The rider wore a black helmet, visor down, impossibly calm as he cut across the center line and rolled right toward them.

Vinny looked up. Confused.

"Yo—?"

The bike drifted to a smooth glide.
The rider's left hand lifted.

Tony's eyes widened. "DOWN!"

Too late.

Muzzle flashes stuttered in the morning light—bright, violent sparks spitting from a suppressed MAC-11 strapped to the rider's forearm. Bullets ripped across the storefront.

Vinny's chest burst open, his phone spinning into the street.

One of the sweepers was thrown backward, broom skittering across concrete.

Joey Fingers screamed and dove behind a metal table, but the rounds chewed through it like paper. His body kicked twice, then slumped sideways, eyes still wide in shock and disbelief.

Tony spun to run.

The rider corrected his aim.

Rounds hammered Tony's back, punching him to the ground. The espresso cup shattered beside him, brown liquid mixing with the blood fanning across the sidewalk.

The motorcycle didn't stop.

It drifted past the dying men with a silent elegance, spraying one last controlled burst into the glass windows of the shop—shattering them into glittering rain. Then it roared away, disappearing down the block before the first alarm on a nearby building even registered.

For a long moment, the world was still again.

Just the hiss of a leaking espresso machine inside the shop.
Just the faint rattle of broken glass settling.
Just Tony Lucio, leader of a dwindling Italian crew, gasping through a final wet breath.

Across the street, an old homeless man peeked out from behind a dumpster, eyes wide, blanket clutched to his chest. He watched the bike vanish, then stared at the bodies sprawled across the sidewalk.

He'd tell no one.
Because people who survived in this neighborhood learned early:
when death comes fast, quiet, and deliberate…

…it's best to pretend you didn't see a damn thing.

But the city would hear about it soon enough.

Three dead Italian bosses in broad daylight.

A coordinated hit delivered with military precision.

A message written in blood that would echo through every crime family from Houston to New Orleans.

And somewhere across town—still oblivious, still living like the world hadn't changed yet—DJ King's empire was waking up.

Not knowing that by nightfall, the streets would be in open revolt…
and the hunt for **LJ King** would inflame the entire city.

CHAPTER 4 – CREAM AT CLUB SPLIT

Night returned to Houston like it had something to prove—loud, bright, and hungry.

Club Split vibrated in the center of it, lights slicing the dark, bass rolling like thunder trapped underground.

Upstairs, far from the sweat and pulse of the dancefloor, Jasmine King crossed her legs behind her desk and checked the time. Her dress shimmered each time she moved, a quiet reminder she never had to speak to own the room. Beside the bar, James twirled an empty tumbler between his fingers, impatient energy bleeding from him like static.

"You sure he's coming?" James asked.

"He'll come," Jasmine said, adjusting her earrings. "Marco Flores never turns down a meeting with a King."

James snorted. "Yeah, especially not *you*."

Before Jasmine could reply, the door swung open.

Marco Flores stepped in wearing confidence like a tailored suit. Jacket crisp, chain gleaming, expression sharp with curiosity and caution.

"Alright," Marco said. "Why am I here? Thought you two wanted my brother."

"Normally we would," James said, walking over to pour a drink. "But tonight's a little different."

Jasmine rose slowly, offering Marco a smile that suggested she held half the city in her palm. "I wanted to speak with you first."

Marco sat without being asked—somewhere between respect and arrogance. He accepted the drink James offered, tossed it back, and exhaled.

"Okay," he said. "Talk."

Jasmine clasped her hands, almost polite. "Me and my brother are expanding our operations. We're interested in buying all three of your father's clubs."

Marco blinked. "Buying? Not partnering?"

"Buying," James repeated. "Outright."

Jasmine nodded. "And we're prepared to pay three times their actual value."

Marco laughed—short, surprised, impressed. "Three times? Damn. You two must really love nightclubs."

James's eyes glinted. "We don't give a damn about nightclubs. We care about opportunity."

He reached into his pocket, pulling out a tiny glass vial filled with soft, off-white powder. It looked harmless, like powdered sugar.

"And this," he said, lifting it between two fingers, "is our opportunity."

He tossed it to Marco, who caught it reflexively.

"What's this?" Marco asked, rolling it between his fingertips.

"The future," Jasmine said.

Marco cracked it open, sniffed it, debated—and then poured a neat line across the back of his hand.

Jasmine raised a brow. "Already feeling brave, huh?"

Marco smirked and inhaled.

The effect hit fast.

His pupils widened. Shoulders loosened. A buzzing energy rippled through him—clean, sharp, euphoric. His nerves hummed like someone had plugged him into a brighter version of himself.

"Oh damn," Marco whispered. "That's not coke."

"No," James said, satisfied. "It's called Cream. Ten times cleaner than molly. No crash. No shakes. No paranoia. Just a perfect high."

Jasmine stepped closer, voice smooth as silk. "And we want to push it through your family's clubs. You bring atmosphere, influence, and reach. We bring the product."

Marco looked at his hands again—like seeing them for the first time. "I feel incredible," he admitted, almost to himself. "Like... clear."

"That's what everyone's going to pay for," Jasmine said. "Clarity."

For a moment, it looked like Marco might say yes. The high glowed through him. The money was staggering. The pitch was perfect.

But then reality crept back into his eyes.

He closed the vial carefully and handed it back.

"I'd sell to you for three times the value," Marco said. "Gladly. But I can't."

James set the glass down a little too hard. "Why not?"

"Because my father would never go for it," Marco said. "Those clubs wash half his money. They're not just businesses—they're pipes. You don't sell your pipes."

Silence tightened around the room.

Jasmine inhaled slowly, containing her disappointment with the grace of someone trained from birth to hide the blade in her smile.

"We appreciate your honesty," she said.

Marco stood, buttoning his jacket. "And hey—thanks for the sample. I'm keeping that."

James's jaw ticked. Jasmine gestured permission without blinking.

Marco grinned like a man who didn't understand he was stepping off a cliff. "Tonight's on me then. I'm about to feel this in VIP."

He chuckled his way out of the office.

When the door closed, James turned to Jasmine, frustration simmering under his calm.

"Well?" he said. "Plan B?"

Jasmine didn't move. Didn't blink. Didn't breathe for a moment.

Then she exhaled, her expression sharpening into something cold and strategic.

"Call Roxy," she said. "And tell her to start taking notes."

James lifted a brow. "Notes for what?"

"For who replaces the Flores family," Jasmine said quietly. "Because if they won't sell…"

Her eyes slid toward the window overlooking the dancefloor.

"…we'll make room for someone who will."

CHAPTER 5 – ROXY'S JOB

VIP at Club Split glowed pink and gold, a velvet womb pumped full of money and music. Champagne bottles lined the walls like trophies; LED lights washed over half-naked dancers and the rich men who pretended they weren't being hunted by their own greed.

Roxy moved through the room like smoke.

Long legs, red hair, a silver dress that clung to her like it wanted to confess every crime she'd ever committed. She carried no weapon—at least none anyone could see. Her smile was soft and devastating. Her eyes were knives.

Marco Flores didn't stand a chance.

He lounged on the velvet couch surrounded by bottles, the Cream still sparking through his nervous system, making everything feel clearer, louder, sexier.

When Roxy slid into his lap, he welcomed her with open hands.

"Well, hello," Marco murmured, running a palm along her thigh. "Jasmine sent you?"

Roxy tilted her head, lips brushing his ear. "Something like that."

Her voice was warm honey. Her touch was soft sin.

But behind her eyes, the job had already begun.

Marco nuzzled her neck, laughing under his breath. "You are perfect, baby. What's your name?"

"Roxy," she said.

He grinned. "Of course it is."

The champagne room around them blurred—men cheering, dancers spinning, the bass vibrating the floors. Marco let his head fall back as Roxy kissed down his jawline, then slid her lips to his ear.

"You're tense," she whispered.

"What? Me?" Marco laughed. "I feel amazing."

"That's good," Roxy said. "I want you relaxed."

She shifted on his lap, straddling him fully now, her hands sliding behind his head. Marco's breathing deepened, fingertips digging into her waist as he leaned into her.

Roxy lowered her mouth to his, slow, sensual—

Then she flipped.

In one smooth movement she pressed her chest to his, lips at his ear, her body pinning him down so he couldn't move. Marco gasped in surprise, half aroused, half off-balance.

"What are you—"

Her lips brushed his earlobe.

Then her mouth opened.

Marco froze.

Something thin and metallic glimmered between her teeth.

Before he could process it, Roxy slipped a razor blade from her mouth with her tongue—slick, silent, deadly.

Marco's eyes went wide.

"R—Roxy—"

"Shh," she whispered.

With one swift, practiced motion, she dragged the blade across his throat—clean, deep, perfect.

Marco's breath caught in his lungs, then erupted in a wet choke. Blood pulsed hot against Roxy's chest, spraying her collarbone, staining her silver dress like it was part of the design.

Marco tried to speak, but only gurgles came out.

Roxy held him as he bled, whispering something he couldn't understand, stroking the back of his head like a lover comforting a dying animal.

His body went slack within seconds.

Roxy wiped the blade on his designer jacket and let his corpse slump gently into the couch, head tilted like a man who'd fallen asleep in luxury.

The music outside the champagne room drowned everything.

She stood, adjusted her dress, smoothed her hair, and stepped calmly away from the body. With one swipe of her thumb, she sent Jasmine a text.

Done.

No emoji. No flourish. Just the truth.

Across the club, Jasmine King was mid-conversation with three investors in VIP, champagne flute in hand, smile perfectly effortless. Her phone buzzed.

She glanced at the screen, then tucked it away without expression.

"Anyway," Jasmine said, raising her glass, "as I was saying—our expansion will open doors no one in Houston has ever walked through."

The men nodded, eager, intoxicated by her presence.

And Jasmine kept talking, kept smiling, kept turning the gears of her empire…

…as Marco Flores bled quietly into the cushions upstairs.

CHAPTER 6 – CALLS, CHAMPAGNE, AND A SETUP

The FBI surveillance van sat in the same spot it had occupied all night—half-hidden beneath an oak tree across from the King estate, engine off, condensation fogging the windshields. Inside, Agents Knight and Barber were stiff from waiting, nerves still jangling from the earlier call.

Barber checked the battery level on their listening gear. "We need to take this back for a full sweep. These channels keep dropping."

Knight barely heard him. "One hundred and fifty million," he murmured, shaking his head. "How does somebody even move money like that?"

Barber smirked. "With confidence. Or a gun to their head."

Before Knight could respond, a sharp rap hit the side of the van.

Both agents jumped.

Floodlights from the estate cast a long shadow over the passenger door. Then a familiar face appeared at the window—DJ King's head of security, a brick-built man named Whitlock. Dark suit. Darker expression.

Knight cracked the window an inch. "Can we help

you?"

Whitlock leaned in with a grin that didn't reach his eyes. "Boss wanted to send you boys a gift."

He held up a frosted bottle of champagne—crystalline, expensive, sweating in the night air.

Knight blinked. "Why?"

Whitlock shrugged. "Hospitality. You're guests on his street, right?"

Barber's eyes narrowed. "We're not allowed to accept—"

Whitlock shoved the bottle through the cracked window anyway. "Too bad. You just did."

He tapped the roof twice, turned, and walked back toward the gate without another word.

Knight stared at the bottle in his hands. "This is a threat, right? This feels like a threat."

Barber's voice was low. "Everything from these people is a threat."

Across the street, the King estate glowed warm and golden like nothing in the world was wrong.

Inside, everything was wrong.

In DJ King's private office, heavy bass pulsed through the walls—old-school Houston rap turned up loud enough to rattle the glass in the windows. Speakers in each corner blasted so much low-end that even a whisper became a distortion. No bug on earth was catching this conversation clean.

Lue King stood near the desk, pacing, face tight with anger he was trying—and failing—to control.

DJ poured two drinks, handed one to his brother, and watched him closely. "Alright," he said. "Tell me again. From the start."

Lue drank half the glass at once. "It wasn't just us."

DJ's expression didn't change, but something in the room went still.

Lue continued, voice sharp and furious. "Every major family got hit today. Italian, Dominican, Cartel, the Haitians, those Gulf kids out in Baytown—every one of them woke up bleeding money. Accounts drained. Crypto wallets cleaned out. Stashes vanished."

DJ leaned forward. "How bad?"

Lue stared into his drink like it insulted him. "Across the board? About one-point-five billion."

He said it flat, but the number cracked the air open.

DJ sat back in his chair. "You're sure?"

"I got calls from Marco's people, from Lucio's underboss—before he got ventilated this morning. You ain't the only one missing money. Everybody got robbed."

DJ rubbed his chin, processing. "So this wasn't betrayal. Not internal."

"Nope," Lue said. "This was coordinated. Military-level precision. And they knew exactly where we kept our stuff."

DJ's gaze flicked to the flickering security feed in the corner. "Which means someone on the inside talked."

"Or," Lue countered, "someone's been watching us longer than the Feds."

DJ didn't argue.

He drank instead.

The music thumped on—deep drums, chopped vocals, bass shaking the air—masking everything.

"Alright," DJ said finally. "What's the response from the others?"

Lue exhaled, slow and frustrated. "Everybody's calling for a sit-down. Neutral ground. Mandatory attendance. Italians, Kings, Flores crew, the rest. They wanna prevent a citywide war."

DJ laughed once—cold, humorless. "There already *is* a war. They're just late to announce it."

Lue set his glass down on the desk, leaning forward. "They want you to host."

DJ raised a brow. "Me?"

"You're the one everybody trusts not to run their mouth. Or turn it into a shootout."

DJ considered this, swirling the drink in his hand. Hosting meant power. Hosting meant liability. It meant he was at the center of whatever storm was brewing.

"They want it tomorrow night," Lue added.

DJ took a long breath. "Then tomorrow night, it is."

Lue nodded. "But we need to figure out who the hell did this. Because a billion-five doesn't disappear unless somebody does more than steal. That kind of move? That's somebody declaring they're bigger than all of us."

DJ didn't respond right away.

He stared past his brother, through the window, at the empty stretch of road where the FBI van sat half-hidden under the tree.

"They think they're watching us," DJ said quietly. "Truth is... they ain't got a clue what's coming."

Inside the surveillance van, Barber frowned at the audio waveform. "I swear this is deliberate. The music spiked on every channel. It's scrambling the feed."

Knight opened the champagne box again. Inside, beneath the fancy bottle, lay a folded piece of paper.

His blood chilled.

"Barber," he whispered. "Look."

It was a handwritten note on thick stationery.

Two words:

KEEP LISTENING.

Barber swallowed hard. "He knows exactly what he's doing."

Knight nodded slowly. "Yeah. And he wants us to think we're in control."

They both stared through the windshield toward the glowing estate.

Neither realized the real game wasn't outside the van…

…it was happening inside DJ King's walls, where a billion-dollar war had just begun, and where one missing name—**LJ King**—was about to set all of Houston on fire.

CHAPTER 7 – BASEMENT BAPTISM

The basement beneath Club Split didn't sound like the club above it.

Upstairs: music, laughter, bottles popping.

Down here: concrete, drip water, and the wet slap of fists hitting flesh.

Dre hung from a hook in the ceiling, wrists bound tight with industrial cord. His shoes were already off, his socks soaked in blood from where James's men had beaten his ankles to powder. Two bodyguards—Mondo and Grit—took turns working him over, each punch echoing like a hammer hitting raw meat.

James King watched from a metal chair, elbows on his knees, eyes half-lidded behind wire-frame glasses. He looked less like a crime boss and more like a bored grad student waiting for a lecture to end.

Dre spit blood onto the floor. "Y'all… y'all got the wrong dude, man—"

James flicked his fingers. Grit stepped forward and hit Dre in the ribs so hard his whole body jolted.

"I really hate liars," James said calmly. "We know you've been asking about Cream. We know you've been circling our couriers. We know you've been running your mouth on the East End."

"I wasn't—!"

Mondo backhanded him before he could finish.

James sighed. "Dre, my guy, stop wasting my time. I got, like, twelve meetings tonight."

Dre wheezed, coughing up blood. "I was just… curious, man. That's all."

James stood, stretching his back. "Curiosity is dangerous. Especially about us."

He nodded at his men. "Bring it out."

Mondo rolled a rusted steel barrel from the corner. The lid was already off. A thin chemical mist escaped into the air—sharp, corrosive, wrong. Dre smelled it and immediately panicked.

"Oh hell no—hell **no**—what is that? What is that?!"

James tapped the rim lightly with his knuckles. "Potassium hydroxide. Eats through pretty much anything… except stainless steel."

Dre screamed into the dark basement, voice cracking. "YO PLEASE—PLEASE—JAMES DON'T DO THIS—"

"Relax," James said. "We're not putting you in it. Not yet."

He signaled. Mondo lowered the hook until Dre dangled horizontally over the open barrel, face inches above the swirling caustic liquid.

The liquid hissed as if impatient.

Dre sobbed. "Please—PLEASE—don't do this—"

James leaned in close. "Then stop lying."

A soft pair of heels clicked on the basement steps.

Every man in the room straightened.

Jasmine King descended like the temperature dropping. Black dress. Gloves. Hair in a perfect knot. Her presence alone made the air tighten.

James smiled, stepping back. "Was wondering when you'd show."

"I got sidetracked," Jasmine said, her voice cool and dangerous. "VIP needed attention. Now show me what you've learned."

James gestured at Dre. "He's stalling."

Jasmine approached the barrel, looking Dre dead in the eyes. "You know what bothers me?" she asked softly. "When small men waste my time."

Dre whimpered. "Miss King... please..."

She grabbed his face with one hand, forcing him to look at her. "If you lie to me, I kill you. If you stay silent, I kill you. But if you insult my intelligence?"

Her grip tightened.

"I wipe out your entire bloodline."

James raised a brow. Even he didn't say things like that out loud.

Jasmine nodded at Mondo. He lowered Dre closer until his nose almost kissed the fumes. Dre gagged, eyes wide, skin burning from just the mist.

"START TALKING," Jasmine commanded.

Dre broke instantly. "OKAY—OKAY—OKAY! I wasn't curious! Someone sent me! I was just trying to get info!"

"Who sent you?" Jasmine asked.

Dre hesitated one second too long.

Jasmine pressed his forehead closer. A drop of sweat slid off his cheek and sizzled when it hit the liquid.

"WHO SENT YOU?"

"JAVIER FLORES!" Dre screamed. "Javier! Javier Flores! He— he said—he said y'all were moving something new! Something big! Something he needed to know about!"

Jasmine's expression didn't change, but the air around her did. Cold. Final.

James stepped forward. "You should've just said that the first time."

Dre sobbed. "PLEASE—I told you the truth—please let me go—please I swear I won't—"

James didn't let Jasmine answer.

He drew his gun and shot Dre in the head.

One clean, quiet pop. Dre's body went limp, dangling over the barrel.

Mondo jerked the hook up out of reflex to avoid the corpse dropping in.

Jasmine turned to James slowly.

"Why," she said, "did you do that?"

James shrugged. "He was done talking."

"I wasn't done listening."

James smirked. "He wasn't gonna say anything else. Plus, you're scary enough without the extra theatrics."

The basement fell silent.

Jasmine walked toward her brother, heels echoing. She stopped inches from him.

"Next time," she said quietly, "I decide when they die."

James held up his hands. "Alright, alright. My bad. Heat of the moment."

Jasmine looked back at Dre's dangling corpse. Then at the barrel. Then at her gloves.

"Clean this up," she told the guards. "Burn whatever's left. Nobody outside this room needs to know Javier Flores is probing our operation."

James wiped his glasses on his shirt. "Javier's poking around more than usual. After tonight? We should visit him."

Jasmine nodded, already walking toward the stairs.

"Tomorrow," she said. "Tonight, we celebrate."

"Celebrate what?" James asked.

Jasmine paused on the last step, looking back with a

cold, perfect smile.

"That we're ahead."

CHAPTER 8 – THE COUNCIL OF WOLVES

The warehouse sat on the edge of the Houston Ship Channel—an empty, rust-stained husk that smelled of old salt and forgotten secrets. Tonight, though, it pulsed with danger.

Luxury cars lined the loading dock. Armed men stood shoulder to shoulder along the walls. And in the center of the cavernous space, beneath flickering industrial lights, the city's criminal elite gathered like wolves around a carcass.

DJ King walked in with Lue at his side, both men dressed sharp enough to cut through steel. Conversations softened as they approached. Eyes tracked them the way prey studies predators—or predators study other predators.

Lue scanned the room. "Whole city showed up."

"They didn't have a choice," DJ murmured.

At a long steel table, the bosses were already seated:

Turk Barrington, the Jamaican shot-caller with dreadlocks streaked in gray, gold rings on every finger, and eyes that never blinked.

Benny Jung, the quiet Asian syndicate boss with the stiff posture of a man who'd survived too many gunfights to ever truly relax.

Harvey Eisenstein, the pale Jewish money launderer who handled offshore accounts for half the room and owed favors to the other half.

Javier Flores, leaning back with a predator's smirk, his expensive suit wrinkled from a night he clearly didn't spend at home.

And several underbosses—Italians, Baytown Gulf boys, Haitian lieutenants—restless, angry, armed.

At the head of the table sat an empty chair.

DJ took it.

The noise in the warehouse died completely.

Turk slammed his palm on the table so hard the metal echoed. "Let's not waste time. We all got hit today. Not small either—*big*. Somebody cleaned out every account worth touching."

Javier smirked. "An inside job seems most likely."

Benny Jung's jaw tightened. "Inside of *whose* house?"

Turk turned his hard stare on DJ. "Let's start with the obvious. DJ King… your nephew's name is floating all over the street."

Lue bristled. "Watch your mouth, Turk."

But Turk kept his eyes on DJ.

"LJ King," he repeated. "They say he disappeared two nights ago. They say he had access. And they say he was the only one missing when the money vanished."

Murmurs broke out across the table.

DJ didn't flinch. "My nephew didn't steal from me. And he sure as hell didn't steal from y'all."

Turk leaned in. "Then where is he?"

DJ's silence was short—but heavy.

He didn't know.
And that fact hung in the air like smoke.

Harvey Eisenstein cleared his throat nervously. "We all know the Kings run a tight ship. If LJ was involved, DJ would've already handled it."

"That's what scares me," Benny Jung said quietly. "If DJ didn't sanction this… then someone else is playing games with a billion and a half dollars."

Lue folded his arms. "We're not the enemy here."

"Maybe not," Turk replied. "But until I get proof otherwise, the boy stays on the table."

The tension thickened. DJ's eyes sharpened, but he didn't raise his voice.

"I vouch for my family," DJ said. "My word is law. I don't protect thieves."

The room considered this. In their world, DJ's word held weight. But tonight that weight felt strained—like the floorboards beneath it were cracking.

Then Harvey cleared his throat again. "There's another issue floating around. Something new hitting the street. A drug."

Javier's brows lifted with false innocence.

Harvey continued. "Cream. That's what it's called. Word is, someone out there is moving a designer product unlike anything we've seen."

All eyes slowly shifted to DJ King.

Even Lue looked surprised.

Javier smiled without smiling. "Rumors say the Kings created it."

DJ leaned back, posture loose, voice steady. "Rumors are bullshit. We aren't moving anything new. Whoever's selling Cream is playing their own game."

Turk eyed him. "A new drug shows up the same week we all get robbed? Timing seems odd."

DJ shrugged. "If I was behind a billion-dollar heist, I wouldn't be selling dime bags of candy powder."

A few men smirked. The tension softened slightly.

Javier, though, kept smiling like he knew something nobody else did.

DJ tapped the table with two fingers—sharp, controlled. "Listen. We need unity, not paranoia. Somebody hit every one of us. That means somebody out there thinks we're weak."

He looked each boss in the eye, one by one.

"I'm offering triple product to every family for the next six months. No tax. No skim. Cost only. To stabilize the streets until we catch whoever did this."

The room murmured in approval.

Harvey nodded vigorously. "That'll calm the soldiers down."

Benny Jung folded his hands. "It'll stabilize the clubs."

Turk leaned back, thinking. Finally, he exhaled. "Alright. That's a good gesture."

But Javier Flores tilted his head.

"Generous," he said. "Very generous. Almost like a man trying to hide guilt."

Lue shot up from his chair. "Say that again, Flores. I swear to—"

DJ raised a hand, stopping him cold.

"No blood tonight," DJ said. "Not here."

Javier held DJ's gaze. "I'm not accusing you. I'm only saying that somebody close to you might've betrayed you. And us."

DJ's jaw twitched, the smallest crack in his calm.

He stood slowly. The warehouse fell silent.

"I'll find who did this," DJ said. "And when I do, I'll deliver them to each of you personally. Piece by piece."

The wolves around the table nodded, satisfied—for now.

But as the meeting broke and men drifted into the shadows of the warehouse, one truth settled over DJ

King like a cold weight:

The city believed LJ King was guilty.

And the more DJ denied it...

...the more dangerous the rumor became.

Because in their world, guilt wasn't about the truth.

It was about the story everyone else decided to believe.

CHAPTER 9 – SNIPER ON THE ROOF

The night wind cut across the Port of Houston like a blade—cold, sharp, carrying the metallic tang of shipyard steel and ocean salt. On top of an abandoned packing warehouse two blocks from the meeting site, **Mac King** lay prone behind a long-range rifle, cheek pressed to the stock, breath calm as a prayer.

Mac wasn't loud like Lue.
Wasn't strategic like Jasmine.
Wasn't charming like James.

He was the quiet nephew—the one everyone forgot about until it was already too late.

Through the scope, the warehouse parking lot below looked small, almost delicate. Crime bosses emerged in ones and twos, flanked by their soldiers, each group moving with the kind of tension only betrayal could create.

Mac exhaled slowly.

"Come on," he muttered. "Where you at?"

Then the steel door opened.

Benny Jung stepped into the night air, adjusting his suit jacket, looking both ways before signaling for his driver to bring the car around. The Asian boss seemed relaxed—maybe even relieved the meeting hadn't turned into a massacre.

Mac steadied the crosshairs on Benny's forehead.

A breath in.

A breath out.

Mac squeezed the trigger.

The rifle barked once—low, suppressed, nothing more than a cough against the wind.

Down below, Benny Jung's head snapped back as if yanked by an invisible hook. His body crumpled onto the concrete, blood spilling in a dark arc across the pavement.

For a beat, no one moved.

Then the screaming started.

Guards rushed to Benny's body, weapons drawn, shouting directions in a dozen languages. Car engines revved. Men dove behind bumpers and pillars, searching the rooftops.

Mac was already three steps ahead.

He broke down the rifle with practiced speed, sliding each piece into a black duffel bag. No panic. No wasted motion. Just the cold efficiency he'd been raised on.

By the time the first guards aimed their pistols toward his building, Mac was gone—slipping down a back stairwell into the shadows of the port.

Benny Jung was dead.

And Mac King vanished into the night like a whisper.

Inside the meeting warehouse, the echo of chaos spilled through the walls—shouts, engines roaring, someone yelling that Benny had been hit. Men scrambled toward exits, terrified of becoming the next name on a bullet.

DJ King didn't move.

He stood beside the long steel table, jaw tight, eyes calm, as if the storm outside had nothing to do with him.

Harris, his attorney, hurried over with wide, frantic eyes. "DJ—someone killed Benny. They're saying it was a setup!"

DJ didn't even look up. "Of course it was."

Harris swallowed. "Do you want me to lock down the estate? Or—"

DJ turned to him finally, voice low and steady.

"I want you to find LJ."

Harris blinked. "Sir?"

"Find him," DJ repeated. "By any means. Anyone hiding him? I want names. Anyone helping him? I want them brought to me. I don't care if he stole the money or if someone's framing him—I need my nephew in front of me."

Harris nodded quickly. "Yes, sir. I'll start immediately."

DJ walked toward the center of the warehouse and motioned to one of his men. "Bring the twins."

Minutes later, **Jasmine and James King** entered side by side—both composed, both alert, both still carrying the metallic scent of what they'd done earlier that night.

"Daddy?" Jasmine asked.

James pushed his glasses up. "What's going on? We heard shots."

DJ looked at each of them. "Cream," he said.

They exchanged a subtle glance.

"What about it?" James asked.

"Every family in Houston is asking about it," DJ said. "Somebody's pushing a new product. Rumors say it's ours."

Jasmine's expression didn't flicker. "And you're wondering if there's truth to that rumor."

"I'm wondering," DJ said slowly, "how someone created a drug so powerful it has the whole damn city whispering."

James's tongue pressed against his cheek, hiding a smirk.

DJ stepped closer, lowering his voice so only they could hear.

"If Cream is real," he said, "I want in."

Jasmine folded her arms. "And if it's fake?"

"Find out," DJ said. "Whoever's behind it... they're playing with fire. And if it's profitable?"

The coldest part of Jasmine's mind clicked awake.

"Then it's ours," she said.

DJ nodded once.

Chaos still echoed outside—sirens, tires screeching, guards shouting into radios—but inside DJ King's world, everything sharpened into focus.

Find LJ.
Unmask the thief.
Claim Cream.
Control the war.

He walked toward the exit without looking back.

"Handle it," DJ said.

And the twins, silent and deadly as matching shadows, followed.

CHAPTER 10 – THE FBI BRIEFING

Deputy Director **Stanley Ware** didn't like yelling—he preferred the kind of quiet that made people sweat.

But this morning, the Houston field office was buzzing loud enough to rattle bones: phones ringing, analysts sprinting between desks, agents shouting for updated intel. A war was unfolding in real time, and no one had a map.

Ware stood in the briefing room wearing a navy suit that fit like armor, jaw clenched so tight the muscles pulsed. On the wall behind him, a line of corkboards waited—blank, hungry.

Agents Knight and Barber slipped into the room still smelling faintly of the champagne DJ King's bodyguard had gifted them. They looked exhausted, wired, and uneasy.

"Sit," Ware said without looking up.

They obeyed instantly.

Ware opened a large evidence folder and began laying out glossy eight-by-ten photos one by one. The first three hit the table like body blows.

Tony Lucio.
Joey Fingers.
Vinny the Kid.

All dead. All shot to pieces outside the Lucios' coffee shop.

Knight winced. Barber crossed his arms tightly.

Ware pinned the photos to the first board, the red pushpins punching in with crisp, deliberate clicks.

"Three members of the Lucio crew executed yesterday morning," Ware said. "Professional job. Clean. No shell casings. No witnesses talking."

He reached for another photo.

This one he held longer before pinning it up.

Benny Jung—face half gone, body sprawled across a port-side parking lot, blood soaking the concrete.

"Last night," Ware said flatly, "someone put a round through Benny Jung's skull outside a crime summit. One shot. Long distance. Sniper-level precision."

Knight and Barber exchanged a look—Mac King flashed through both their minds.

Ware continued without pause.

"These murders aren't isolated. They're part of a coordinated collapse of Houston's criminal infrastructure. Someone is hitting every major player at the same time."

Barber exhaled. "This is retaliation for the stolen funds."

Ware turned sharply, eyes narrowed. "Correct, Agent Barber. And here's the part that should scare you."

He lifted another photo from the folder and placed it dead center on the main board.

A younger man.
Sharp eyes.
Easy smile.
DJ King's bloodline unmistakable.

LJ KING.

Knight swallowed. "Sir... you think he stole the money?"

"I don't think," Ware said. "I know."

He tapped the photo once—hard enough to make it sway.

"Two nights ago, LJ King disappeared. The next morning, one-point-five billion dollars in cash, crypto, and illegal offshore funds vanished from a dozen criminal families. All withdrawals were manual. All insider-level accesses. All using codes only one person had."

Knight frowned. "And that one person was..."

Ware stared at LJ's photo like it offended him.

"LJ King is the record keeper for the entire King organization. He tracks every dollar moving in and out of Houston. Cash shipments. Club skims. Launder routes. Crypto wallets. Street taxes. Even off-book collections tied to foreign syndicates."

He let that settle.

Barber sat up straighter. "So if LJ goes down, the

whole operation collapses."

"If he goes down," Ware corrected, "before we reach him, he won't be talking. Someone out there put a sniper on a roof last night. Someone killed Benny Jung. Someone wiped out the Lucios. The streets believe LJ stole their money."

Ware leaned forward, voice darkening.

"If the criminals find him first, they will tear him apart—slowly. And we lose the only witness who can map the entire city's black economy."

Knight rubbed his temples. "Jesus..."

Ware grabbed a red marker and drew a thick circle around LJ's face.

"All major crimes in Houston converge right here," Ware said. "He's the key. He knows everything. And every killer in the city woke up today wanting his head."

He capped the marker with a sharp click.

"I don't care if DJ King is hiding him. I don't care what street code says. I don't care that we're outnumbered. If we don't find LJ King before the wolves do..."

Ware pointed at the photos of dead bosses—

"...Houston bleeds for a decade."

Knight straightened. "What's our next move?"

Ware didn't blink.

"Everything. You two are on LJ King twenty-four hours. Follow every rumor, every cousin, every burner phone, every stolen car. Kick down doors. Wake up the informants. Turn the city upside down."

His voice dropped to a growl.

"Find.
Me.
LJ."

The briefing room fell silent as Ware walked out, leaving Knight and Barber staring at the board—at the bodies stacking up, at the chaos spreading, at the smiling photo of a young man who had no idea the entire underworld had declared war on his name.

Houston was burning from the inside.

And LJ King was the match.

CHAPTER 11 – FAMILY BUSINESS

The King estate was unusually quiet.

Not the tense, electric silence of danger—but the heavy kind, the kind that settles after a funeral even though no one's died yet. DJ King sat alone in his study, lights low, whiskey glowing amber in a crystal glass. Smoke from his cigar curled toward the ceiling in slow, patient spirals.

When the door opened, he didn't turn.

"Come in, son."

James stepped inside, hands in his pockets, glasses catching the warm lamplight. He looked older tonight—not in years, but in responsibility.

"Lue said you wanted to see me."

DJ gestured to the chair across from him. "Sit."

James did.

For a long moment, neither spoke. The fire crackled in the background. The city hummed beyond the windows. Somewhere down the hall, guards moved in practiced patterns.

Then DJ exhaled.

"You've been working hard," he said.

James frowned. "I always do."

"I know," DJ said softly. "That's the problem."

James blinked, unsure what direction this was going.

DJ studied the rim of his glass as if it held a memory. "When you and Jasmine were young... I wasn't here enough."

James cracked a dry smile. "You weren't here *at all*."

DJ let the hit land. He didn't defend himself.

"You kids grew up in a world shaped by my enemies. You learned how to survive before you learned how to be children. And that's on me."

James shifted, uncomfortable. DJ wasn't the type for confessions.

"But I want you to hear something," DJ continued. "Something I should've said a long time ago."

He set the whiskey down and leaned forward.

"You and Jasmine are the future of this family."

James blinked. "Me?"

DJ nodded. "Your sister has the ruthlessness. You have the brains. Together? You two could build an empire bigger than anything I ever touched."

James swallowed. He wasn't often caught off guard, but this... this cracked something inside him.

"Dad... is something wrong with you? Are you—"

"No," DJ said firmly. "I'm not dying. And I'm not stepping down."

A beat. "But succession matters. The streets are changing. Times are changing. And I need this family prepared."

James looked down at his hands.

"You never said any of this before," he murmured.

"I should have," DJ admitted. "But I was too busy running the world to raise my kids."

James let out a slow breath.

For a moment, they were just father and son. No empire. No enemies. No blood on their hands.

Then James lifted his gaze.

"You think LJ did it?"

The question snapped the quiet like glass underfoot.

DJ's jaw tightened. "I don't know."

"He stole one-point-five billion," James said. "They're calling him a ghost. A traitor. A genius. The whole damn city is hunting him."

"And none of that," DJ replied, "sounds like the LJ I know."

James leaned back, thoughtful. "You don't think he had the skill?"

"Oh, he had the skill," DJ said. "I trained him for that. Kept him close. Made him my shadow on purpose."

"Then what doesn't add up?"

DJ's eyes narrowed.

"The motive."

James opened his mouth, then shut it. The math really *didn't* make sense. LJ had money. Access. Power. Protection. The family loved him. DJ trusted him more than half his captains.

And LJ wasn't stupid—stealing from one criminal empire was suicide. Stealing from *all* of them? That was madness.

"So if he didn't do it," James said slowly, "somebody wants us to think he did."

DJ nodded. "And that scares me more than the theft."

James rubbed his jaw. "You think LJ is alive?"

DJ stared out the window at the dark stretch of road.

"He better be," he said. "Because if he's dead... this whole city is about to burn."

James stood, ready to leave, but DJ stopped him.

"Son."

James paused.

"I'm proud of you," DJ said quietly. "And I trust you. More than you think."

James didn't smile, but something softened in his eyes.

"Get some rest," DJ added. "Tomorrow we go hunting."

James nodded and stepped out of the room, closing the door behind him.

DJ sat alone again, staring at LJ's photo on the desk.

He took a slow sip of whiskey.

"Where the hell are you, boy?"

And why did the world suddenly feel like it was collapsing without him?

CHAPTER 12 – TURK'S WAREHOUSE MASSACRE

The warehouse smelled like diesel and damp cardboard—one of Turk Barrington's many off-book distribution hubs tucked behind a scrap yard in south Houston. A dozen of Turk's men were unloading crates from a box truck, laughing, smoking, cursing about the cold. They had no idea death was already perched above them.

On the opposite rooftop, **Mac King** adjusted his grip on a short-barrel rifle and gave a silent hand signal.

His team—four King shooters in matte-black masks—moved into position.

Mac watched the workers below with the detached calm of a surgeon preparing for a cut. No nerves. No questions. Just work.

The truck's back doors burst open.

Mac and his men opened fire.

Silenced rifles spat thunder without thunder—quick, violent bursts. The first row of Turk's crew dropped instantly, bodies folding before their brains registered the shots. Crates shattered. Cigarettes fell from dead fingers. A man screamed as he crawled behind a pallet, only to take a round through the spine.

Pandemonium erupted.

"WE UNDER ATTACK—!"

Another burst cut the scream short.

Mac descended a fire escape ladder as his men pushed forward in coordinated violence. They moved like a single organism—efficient, lethal. Every step someone died.

Turk's men scrambled for weapons. Some fired blindly. Some hid. Some froze completely, paralyzed by the realization that whoever was attacking them knew exactly what they were doing.

Near the loading ramp, Turk himself limped out of the office trailer, dreadlocks bouncing, gold rings flashing under the warehouse lights. He carried a pistol and a machete, stubborn anger carved into his face.

"SHOW YOURSELF!" Turk roared. "COME FACE ME LIKE A MAN!"

Mac shot him in the leg.

Turk's roar became a raw, guttural groan as he crashed to one knee, the pistol clattering away.

Mac approached with the calm of a man walking through his own backyard.

Turk snarled, blood soaking through his pants. "Finish me, boy. Don't dance around it."

Mac didn't blink. "That's above my pay grade."

Turk spit blood onto the concrete. "DJ send you?

Huh? He too scared to do his own killing now?"

A pair of heavy footsteps echoed across the warehouse.

Every remaining King shooter stopped.

Every dying man on the floor went still.

Turk's eyes widened despite himself.

DJ King walked in through the open loading doors —slow, deliberate, dressed in a dark overcoat that looked more like a judge's robe than a crime boss's attire. He moved with the authority of a man who believed the building belonged to him, not Turk.

Mac stepped aside.

Turk kept his chin high even as blood dripped down his chin. "DJ," he growled. "Brother... you come to kill me yourself?"

DJ didn't answer. He walked past corpses, stepping carefully around blood as if avoiding puddles after a storm. He stopped directly in front of Turk, hands in his pockets, expression unreadable.

"You put a bounty on my nephew," DJ said quietly.

Turk laughed hoarsely. "Your boy stole from everyone. I'm cleaning up the mess you too blind to admit."

DJ tilted his head. "You put a bounty on *family*."

Turk spat. "Family ain't immunity. Family ain't God. You know that."

DJ lowered into a crouch so their eyes aligned.

"You made your move," DJ said. "Now I make mine."

Turk grinned, teeth bloody. "Do it then. Don't give me speeches."

DJ smiled faintly. "I'm not giving a speech."

He drew a revolver—classic, polished steel—and pressed the barrel gently to the center of Turk's forehead.

Turk bared his teeth. "You Kings think you own Houston."

DJ met his stare.

"We do."

He pulled the trigger.

The shot echoed like a closing door.

Turk's body collapsed sideways, eyes open but empty, blood spreading into a dark halo around his head.

DJ stood and holstered the revolver.

Mac stepped forward. "What now, Unc?"

DJ scanned the warehouse—stacks of product, pallets of cash, weapons, ledgers, chemicals, crates with unmarked stamps. A fortune of illegal enterprise laid bare.

"Now," DJ said calmly, "you clean."

Mac nodded.

"And the inventory?" he asked.

DJ clasped Mac's shoulder—firm, approving.

"Whatever you find down here," DJ said, "you keep. Payment for loyalty. Payment for silence."

Mac tried not to smile, but it showed anyway.

DJ glanced one last time at Turk's corpse.

"Burn the rest," he said. "Let Houston smell what betrayal costs."

And as DJ walked out of the warehouse into the humid night, the echo of gunfire still fading behind him, a new truth settled over the city:

The war wasn't coming.

It had already begun.

CHAPTER 13 – FUNERAL HOME LOGISTICS

The King Family Funeral Home sat on the corner of Lyons Avenue, its brick walls washed in soft amber light, the sign out front flickering like it was too tired to advertise death anymore. At night, the place felt older than the city—quiet, patient, and full of secrets.

James King parked in the back, stepping out into the cool air. He adjusted his glasses, straightened his hoodie, and headed toward the service entrance.

The door cracked open before he could knock.

Uncle Wesley King filled the doorway, tall and lean, eyes soft with age but sharp beneath it. He wore a black suit that somehow looked both professional and criminal.

"James," Wesley said, smiling just enough. "Come on in, boy."

Inside, the funeral home smelled faintly of lilies, disinfectant, and cold marble. Wesley led James down a hallway lined with framed photos of past generations—old men in sharper suits, women with hard eyes and church hats. The King family had buried half the city over the years, and Wesley had learned from them all.

They stepped into the embalming prep room.

Stainless-steel tables. Cabinet doors. Supplies neatly arranged. But on the center table tonight sat something new:

Two boxes of **Cream**, each sealed and taped.

Wesley tapped the lid with a latex glove. "This what's got everybody's panties in a twist?"

James smirked. "Something like that."

Wesley gave a low whistle. "Jasmine tell me it hits cleaner than coke and twice as long."

"Ten times," James corrected lightly. "No crash either."

Wesley raised a brow. "Boy... y'all really out here making superpowers."

James shrugged, trying to play it cool but unable to hide his pride. "Product this hot doesn't stay local. We need new routes—quiet ones."

Wesley chuckled and motioned toward the garage.

They walked through a sliding door into the vehicle bay. Three polished black hearses sat in a row, chrome gleaming under the fluorescents.

"Perfect cover," Wesley said. "Nobody wants to open a casket unless they're getting paid or traumatized."

James nodded. "We need to hit Miami and Vegas first. High-end markets. Heavy nightlife. Guaranteed turnover."

Wesley grinned. "You know... I wasn't always an undertaker."

James gave him a look. "Yeah, I've heard stories."

Wesley raised both brows. "Stories? Son, I had whole *eras*."

James laughed despite the stress of the week. "So you're good to move it?"

Wesley walked to the nearest hearse, opened the back door, and slid out a gleaming, empty casket. He knocked on the metal lid.

"These beauties ride right through TSA checkpoints at private airports," Wesley said. "Then they get picked up by my partners on the other end. Miami's handled by a pastor who owes me a kidney. Vegas... well, the less you know the better."

James nodded approvingly. "We'll pack the Cream in the cavity beneath the lining. No dog hits, no scanners picking anything up?"

Wesley smirked. "I've been hiding things from cops since before you were born, nephew. Only difference now is the product doesn't scream or bleed."

James exhaled with relief. "Good. We need the first shipment out by Friday. Jasmine's meeting with buyers in Miami. I'll handle Vegas personally."

Wesley stepped forward and placed a hand on James's shoulder.

"You're doing good, son," Wesley said quietly. "Your father built the empire. You and your sister are expanding it. Proud of y'all."

James looked away, uncomfortable with praise but warmed by it. "We're just trying to keep the family ahead."

Wesley closed the casket lid gently.

"Cream leaving Houston is a big move," he said. "Once it's out there… you can't pull it back in."

James nodded.

"That's the point."

Wesley smiled, showing a flash of gold tooth. "Then let the bodies roll."

James chuckled. "Let's hope we don't have to use any real ones."

Wesley winked. "Nephew, with this kind of money? Bodies are guaranteed."

They sealed the first crate, slid it into the hearse, and locked the door.

Cream was officially going interstate.

And the King empire—quietly, methodically—was becoming something far more dangerous than Houston had ever seen.

CHAPTER 14 – MASSAGE PARLOR CONSPIRACY

The massage parlor sat behind a nail salon on Bellaire, its neon sign flickering like a secret only the wealthy and corrupt understood. Inside, the lights were dim, the air warm, and the smell of eucalyptus fought a losing battle against expensive cologne and cigar smoke.

Behind a beaded curtain, **Lue King** lay face-down on a padded table, his broad back glistening with oil as a topless masseuse worked slow circles into his shoulders. Next to him, separated by only a thin bamboo divider, **Harvey Eisenstein** sprawled on his own table, glasses folded neatly on a chair, another masseuse sitting on his lower back while kneading his spine.

Soft music drifted through hidden speakers—something meant to calm the soul.

But nothing about the conversation was calming.

"You hear about Turk yet?" Lue asked lazily, not lifting his head.

"I heard," Harvey said. "DJ shot him himself, yes?"

"Mhm." Lue smiled into the face cradle. "Didn't even hesitate. Man's been tense for years. This war's good for him."

Harvey chuckled. "War is good for all of us, Lue. As long as we're the ones writing the script."

The masseuse leaned harder into Harvey's back, coaxing a groan from him. Lue cracked his neck to the side, relaxing deeper into the table.

"Javier's next," Lue said casually. "DJ doesn't know it yet, but he'll take him out before the weekend. That man's ego is a liability."

"And DJ thinks Javier is the problem," Harvey said. "Not the real enemy."

Lue grinned. "That's the beauty, Harv. My brother handles the dirty work, and he doesn't even know it."

Harvey let out a pleased hum. "Just like we planned."

A moment of silence passed, broken only by the rhythmic glide of hands over muscle.

Harvey finally spoke again, quieter, more intimate.

"How is the boy?"

Lue's voice softened in a way that would have surprised anyone in DJ's circle.

"Safe," he said. "Doing good. In your world, as we agreed."

Harvey nodded, eyes closed. "LJ fits in nicely. Quiet. Disciplined. Good with numbers."

"He always was," Lue said. "Just like his mama."

Harvey hesitated. "Does he understand what he's

part of?"

Lue's smile faded into something heavier, more paternal.

"No," he admitted. "Not yet. He thinks he's hiding. Thinks he's protecting the family. Thinks he's a ghost in the wind."

Harvey raised a brow, even as the masseuse slid her hands down his ribs.

"And when he learns the truth?"

Lue inhaled deeply, the knot in his back finally releasing. His tone dropped to a soft, cold certainty.

"He'll understand someday. He's my blood. He'll see why it had to be done."

Harvey shifted on the table, fingers drumming lightly against the leather padding.

"The city believes he stole a billion-five on his own," Harvey said. "Quite impressive for a kid who wasn't supposed to leave the accounting office."

Lue chuckled. "People see what we want them to see."

"And DJ..." Harvey said with a smirk. "...is behaving exactly as predicted."

Lue nodded without hesitation.

"He's pissed. Embarrassed. Off balance. And when DJ is off balance, he kills everything in front of him. Turks, Italians, Benny... hell, he might take out Javier just because the man looks at him funny."

Harvey adjusted his head on the pillow, satisfied. "Meaning our competition is dying at the hands of the most feared man in Houston—and we aren't firing a single shot."

Lue exhaled with pleasure as the masseuse dug into a tight muscle near his spine.

"Harv... my brother has been cleaning the city for us since the minute LJ vanished. And by the time he realizes who really took the money..."

Harvey finished the thought with a smile.

"...the empire will already be ours."

Lue chuckled, a low, affectionate sound.

"And DJ will have no choice but to give it to us."

The masseuses continued their work, unaware—or perfectly aware—of the conspiracy stretched out beneath their fingers.

Harvey closed his eyes again.

"Call me sentimental," he murmured, "but I do hope the boy stays loyal."

"He will," Lue said. "He'll hate me at first. Maybe for years."

A pause.

"But he'll understand in the end."

Outside, a police siren wailed down Bellaire.

Inside, Lue and Harvey relaxed under warm hands—two men at peace while the city bled for their ambition.

And far away, hidden behind Harvey's carefully constructed shell companies, **LJ King** remained unaware that the "search" for him was nothing more than the opening move in his father's quiet takeover.

CHAPTER 15 – LJ AND MICHELLE

Harvey Eisenstein's suburban hideaway didn't look like a sanctuary.

It looked like a catalog home—white walls, clean lines, expensive furniture chosen by someone who believed taste could be purchased.

But upstairs, behind a door Harvey never opened without knocking, **LJ King** lay on his back in a bed too soft for a man raised in DJ's world. And **Michelle**, Harvey's much younger wife, straddled him lazily, moving with the absentminded rhythm of someone drifting between pleasure and high.

The lamp cast warm amber across her skin. Music hummed low from a speaker somewhere under the bed. Outside, wind brushed the windows like fingers.

Michelle leaned forward, her breath warm on LJ's collarbone. "You always get this quiet after," she whispered. "What's going through that pretty head of yours?"

LJ stared at the ceiling, chest rising and falling slowly. "Thinking about life," he murmured. "Thinking about what it costs to breathe in this country."

Michelle smiled crookedly and reached for the

nightstand. She dipped a manicured fingernail into a tiny vial and tapped a soft dusting of powder onto her tongue.

LJ watched. "You're doing that again?"

She winked. "It's not coke, baby. It's cleaner."

She offered him the vial.

LJ hesitated only a second before tapping a small taste onto his fingertip. The hit was subtle—quick clarity, a warm lift behind the eyes.

"What is this?" he asked.

"Cream," Michelle said. "Hottest thing in Houston right now. Harvey's chemists are obsessed with it. They're trying to crack the formula."

LJ froze.

Michelle didn't notice. She slid down beside him, draping an arm across his chest. "You ever try the real stuff? Before all this crazy money went missing?"

LJ's thoughts sharpened dangerously. He turned his face toward hers. "Why's Harvey trying to replicate it?"

Michelle shrugged. "He says whoever controls Cream controls half the damn city. And if Harvey controls it... well..."

She traced a finger down LJ's stomach.

"...that means you and me get to eat good forever."

LJ exhaled slowly, trying not to reveal the hit of panic pulsing behind his ribs.

Michelle smiled slyly. "But the chemists can't get it right. There's always a twitch, or a crash, or something off. They keep saying the original batch had a signature they can't replicate. Some genius behind it."

LJ cursed himself for relaxing, for slipping, but the Cream made honesty feel like gravity—inevitable.

"It wasn't a lab," he said quietly. "It was James."

Michelle's hand froze.

LJ blinked, realizing too late what he'd just said.

Michelle's expression smoothed into something unreadable. "James King? Your cousin James?"

LJ rubbed his face. "Forget I said anything."

Michelle didn't blink. "So he's the creator."

LJ sat up a little. "Michelle, I'm serious. Forget it. I shouldn't have—"

She touched his lips gently. "Relax. I don't snitch."

But her eyes were no longer warm—they were calculating, storing the information somewhere deep.

LJ lay back down, the ceiling spinning slightly. Michelle curled against him again, fingers idly tracing patterns on his skin.

"You were talking earlier," she said softly. "About the

American Dream. About Black men. What did you mean?"

LJ let the words rise from somewhere honest and tired.

"People tell us the Dream is out there," he said. "But for men like me? The Dream ain't a ladder... it's a leash. They tell you to work twice as hard, be twice as clean, stay twice as humble just to get half as far. And when you finally make it? They hate you for standing where they said you could go."

Michelle listened quietly.

"That's why I kept the books," LJ said. "It wasn't loyalty to the streets. It was survival. Math made sense. Math didn't lie. People did."

Michelle rested her chin on his chest. "And now?"

"Now the whole damn city thinks I stole from them."

Michelle stroked his jaw with her thumb. "Did you?"

LJ didn't answer.

Not because he couldn't.

Because the truth hurt too much—*and the lie hurt more.*

Michelle kissed him softly. "You're safe here," she whispered.

LJ closed his eyes.

He didn't see the way her gaze drifted toward the nightstand where the Cream vial sat—

or how her mind worked in silence, connecting dots, filing away names, power structures, and opportunities.

Outside the window, the wind pushed harder.

Inside, tucked under Harvey Eisenstein's roof, **LJ King had no idea that the person lying beside him might be the first to sell him out.**

CHAPTER 16 – JASMINE VS. HA JUNG

Club Split was humming beneath her—bass rolling like a heartbeat, lights strobing across hundreds of bodies—but Jasmine King's office stood in its usual pocket of quiet power. Soft jazz. Dim lights. Papers arranged like weapons. Jasmine in a white silk blouse that made her look more like a CEO than a criminal.

She was signing off on Miami distribution invoices when the office door **exploded inward**.

The hinges didn't even get a chance to scream.

Ha Jung, Benny Jung's son, stormed in, eyes wild and wet, a pistol shaking in his hand.

"You bitch!" he screamed. "You killed my father!"

Jasmine didn't flinch. She didn't even sit back. She capped her pen delicately.

"Ha," she said, voice smooth as glass. "You're tracking dirt across my carpet."

He pointed the gun at her chest with both trembling hands. "Don't act calm! I know it was you. My father dies, and your family is the only one that benefits! You set him up!"

Jasmine slowly leaned back in her chair, crossing her legs. "You sure you want to do this in my office?"

"I'm not leaving," he spat. "Not until—"

He never finished the sentence.

Beneath Jasmine's desk—hidden by a panel of carved wood—her finger had already slipped under the lip of a mounted **sawed-off tactical shotgun**.

She squeezed the trigger.

BOOM.

The blast was thunder inside the small room. Ha Jung screamed as his leg exploded beneath him, bone cracking, muscle shredding. He collapsed onto the floor, dropping his gun as blood poured across Jasmine's pristine rug.

He writhed, clutching what was left of his thigh.

"AHHH—AHH—FUCK—FUCK—JASMINE—PLEASE—"

Jasmine stood, calm, collected, brushing a stray fleck of blood off her blouse.

"You storm into my office," she said, circling him like a disappointed teacher, "screaming, pointing a gun at my heart… and you didn't even check under the desk?"

Ha Jung tried to crawl backward, sobbing. "My father—Benny—he didn't deserve that—"

"No," Jasmine agreed softly. "But power never asks what anyone deserves."

She placed her heel on his bleeding leg.

He screamed so loud the windows trembled.

"Shh," she whispered, leaning in. "This is business, Ha. And you pointing a gun at me? That made it personal."

She reached into her drawer, pulled out a stack of documents, and let them fall beside his face.

**TRANSFER OF OWNERSHIP
FOR ALL JUNG FAMILY CLUB PROPERTIES
TO JAMES KING & JASMINE KING**
— No compensation required.

Ha Jung blinked through tears. "W-wh—no—never—"

Jasmine pressed her heel down harder. Blood bubbled around his wound.

"You're done," she whispered. "Your father is gone. Your crew is leaderless. Your suppliers abandoned you the moment he hit the concrete."

Ha Jung cried out, face pressed to the floor.

Jasmine crouched beside him, beautiful and terrifying.

"You have two options, Ha," she said gently. "Sign the papers… or die here and now. Either way, the clubs become ours. But only one option lets you crawl out alive."

Ha Jung sobbed into the carpet.

"Please…"

She shoved a pen into his hand.

"Sign."

His hand shook violently, but he scribbled his name across every line.

Jasmine watched, expression blank, as if observing a child complete homework.

When he finished, she took the papers, flipped through them, nodded once.

Then she stepped off his leg.

"You can crawl out now," she said.

Ha Jung looked up, confused. "W-what?"

"I said crawl." Her voice cooled another degree. "You came in on your feet. You leave on your hands."

He dragged himself across the floor, leaving a long smear of blood behind him. When he reached the door, he looked back once—a broken young man staring at the woman who ruined him.

Jasmine waved a hand dismissively. "Next time, knock."

He disappeared down the hall, screaming for help.

Jasmine closed the door, exhaled, and dialed James.

"It's done," she said.

James replied, half a laugh in his voice, "He sign everything?"

"All of it."

"Damn," James said. "You're better at this than I am."

Jasmine looked at the blood on her rug.

"I know," she said.

Then she poured herself a drink, lit a candle, and went right back to business.

CHAPTER 17 – JAVIER'S FEAR

Javier Flores' estate sat on five manicured acres in Sugar Land, a gaudy fortress of white stone, imported palm trees, and the kind of security system meant to soothe wealthy cowards into feeling powerful.

Tonight, Javier was anything but soothed.

He paced across his marble living room barefoot, half a drink sloshing in his hand. His silk shirt hung open, exposing a gold chain and a chest slick with stress sweat. The overhead chandelier reflected in the liquor each time he lifted the glass, making it shimmer like a warning.

"I don't like this," Javier muttered. "Benny Jung gets sniped, Turk gets wiped out, the Italians are in shambles—DJ's losing his mind."

On the leather sofa, **Lue King** lounged like he owned the house, one ankle over his knee, cigar smoke drifting lazily from his lips. **Harvey Eisenstein** sat beside him, posture relaxed, adjusting his glasses as if this were a board meeting and not a criminal meltdown.

"Relax, Javier," Lue said. "DJ's not losing his mind. He's *reacting*. Big difference."

"That's supposed to make me feel better?" Javier snapped, pacing faster. "The man killed half my competition in forty-eight hours!"

Harvey nodded approvingly. "Exactly as planned."

Javier turned on him. "Planned? My father built an empire. I'm not trying to lose it because DJ King suddenly feels emotional."

Lue chuckled, low and amused. "DJ doesn't do emotional. He does strategic rage. He's cleaning house for us."

Javier swallowed another gulp of his drink, nearly choking. "For *you*, maybe. He hates me."

"DJ hates everybody," Lue said. "But he hates traitors more. As long as you look innocent, he won't touch you."

That reassurance didn't land.

In fact, Javier's hands began to tremble.

He set his drink down and moved to the tall windows, staring out at the moonlit lawn like someone might sprint toward the house with a rifle any second.

"What about Cream?" Javier asked quietly. "We don't know who created it. We don't know how it's moving so fast. We don't know who's distributing. That drug is the most dangerous variable in Houston right now."

Harvey glanced at Lue with a subtle smirk.

Lue kept his tone smooth. "Javier, you're thinking too small."

"Small?" Javier barked. "Cream is already poking holes in every club margin we have! If the Kings are behind it, they'll control half the city by summer."

Harvey folded his hands. "We don't know that the Kings created Cream."

"But we know they're tied to it somehow," Javier muttered. "We have to be proactive. Get ahead of it."

Lue picked a piece of cigar ash from his pants. "Cream ain't your problem. DJ is. Once DJ's out of the picture, the city resets."

Javier's breath caught. He lowered himself onto the arm of a chair.

"You really think your brother can be… removed?"

Harvey smiled. "Every king falls. Even King King."

Lue's eyes darkened, but he didn't deny it.

Before Javier could respond, the doors to the room swung open and **Juan Flores**, his younger cousin, rushed in looking pale.

"Javi," Juan said out of breath. "We have a situation."

Javier's heart pounded. "What now?"

"It's Marco," Juan said. "No one's seen him since yesterday."

Javier stiffened. "What do you mean no one's seen him?"

"Last sighting was… at Club Split."

The silence in the room turned suffocating.

Javier swallowed, voice cracking. "The Kings?"

Juan didn't answer. He didn't have to.

Javier pressed a shaking hand to his forehead. "Oh God... if they touched him, if they laid a finger on my blood—"

Lue rose smoothly from the sofa, brushing ash off his shirt. "Javier, you gotta hold it together. Panic makes mistakes. And mistakes get men buried."

But Javier was already unraveling, pacing again, running his hands through his hair.

"I need Cream," he muttered. "I need control of it. If the Kings are behind it, they'll bury us. If they're not... then someone else is about to become a king of this city."

Harvey stood, gently adjusting his suit jacket. "Focus on the mission. DJ will be isolated soon. Distracted. Paranoid. When he collapses, you'll be in position to take the reins."

Javier stopped pacing.

His eyes flicked between Lue and Harvey.

"You're sure DJ won't come after me before then?"

Lue placed a heavy hand on Javier's shoulder.

"If he does," Lue said, "he won't live long enough to regret it."

Javier exhaled shakily. "Okay. Okay."

But his body was trembling. His drink, still half-full

on the table, vibrated with every unsteady breath.

He was a man desperate for control.
Desperate for certainty.
Desperate to stay alive.

And in the shadows of his gaudy mansion, the two men he trusted most were smiling inside.

Because Javier Flores had no idea—

The Kings weren't his enemies.

His allies were.

CHAPTER 18 – THE STRIPPER ASSASSINS

Javier Flores' estate glittered under the moonlight—gold-framed windows, marble steps, manicured hedges, and enough security cameras to make the Secret Service jealous.

But the gate guard didn't question beauty.

Not when it arrived in the form of **four women in short dresses**, heels clicking like promises, hair perfect even in the evening wind.

At the front of the group stood **Roxy**.

She waved sweetly at the camera as the guard buzzed them in.

A few minutes later, a knock echoed through the mansion.

Javier opened the door himself—shirt half-buttoned, frustration still clinging to him from Lue and Harvey's visit.

The moment he saw them, his mood shifted.

"Well damn," Javier said, flashing a grin. "What do I owe this blessing?"

Roxy smiled innocently. "Sorry to bother you, Mr. Flores. Our van broke down on the way to a bachelor party. We saw your lights... figured we'd come ask for help."

Behind her, the other women shifted their weight, shivering slightly as if they'd been out in the cold too long.

Javier's ego swelled like a bruise.

"My security can take a look," he said. "Why don't you ladies come in while they do?"

Roxy bit her lip. "You sure it's okay?"

"Oh, I insist," Javier said.

Inside, **Juan Flores** sat on the couch with a video game paused on the screen. He perked up instantly when the women entered.

"Damn," Juan whispered. "This is better than Uber Eats."

Javier elbowed him, then gestured the women inside. "Juan, get some drinks. Top-shelf. Make our guests comfortable."

Roxy and her team moved with practiced ease, admiring the décor, touching his expensive furniture, feigning innocence.

Outside, Javier's two guards approached the stranded van.

The moment the door popped open—
pfft pfft
Silenced rounds snapped out from the shadows.

Both guards dropped where they stood, eyes open and empty before they hit the driveway.

One of Roxy's backup shooters emerged from behind

the van, dragged the bodies onto the grass, and melted into the night.

Inside, Javier and Juan sprawled on the sectional while the women laughed, poured drinks, and moved to the soft music playing overhead.

Roxy sat on Javier's lap, her perfume like warm sugar and bad intentions.

"So," she purred, "you were having a hard night?"

Javier sighed, placing a hand on her hip. "You could say that."

"We're good at making men forget their problems," she murmured.

Juan chimed in, swirling his liquor. "Amen to that."

The four women shared a glance.

A tiny one.

Noticeable only if you knew death.

Roxy's hand slid down Javier's chest.

Another assassin leaned forward, brushing Juan's cheek.

Then—

four silver pistols appeared like magic from garters and handbags.

Javier's eyes went wide.

"Wait—"

pfft pfft pfft pfft

Four synchronized shots.

Silencers hissed.

Javier's head snapped back against the couch, a small red blossom blooming on his temple.

Juan didn't even have time to scream—his body jerked once as a round slipped cleanly through his eye.

The music kept playing.

One of the assassins stepped around the couch and delivered a finishing shot to the side of Javier's skull, ensuring there'd be no gasping final act.

Roxy stood, brushing her dress smooth as if nothing had happened.

"Check the halls," she whispered.

The women moved briskly, silent as cats—clearing the kitchen, foyer, and dining room. No movement. No survivors. The guards outside had been the only real obstacle.

Roxy approached Javier's phone on the coffee table.

Harvey Eisenstein
16 Missed Calls

Roxy smirked.

"Sorry, Harvey," she murmured. "Wrong time to hope for help."

She slipped her finger across the screen, letting it lock again.

Then the women gathered near the back door.

Roxy looked once more at the bodies slumped on the couch—two powerful Flores men reduced to warm meat on expensive leather.

"Pack it up, ladies," she said. "We're ghosts."

The team moved out into the night, heels tapping softly on marble, disappearing through the side gate before anyone realized the estate was dead silent.

No alarms.

No shouting.

Only the faint hum of Javier's untouched sound system and the slow drip of blood down his couch.

By the time the house staff discovered the scene at dawn, Roxy's crew would be miles away.

And with Javier dead—

the Flores empire had no head.

Exactly as Lue and Harvey intended.

CHAPTER 19 – THE PARLOR TRAP

The Parlor sat on the edge of Chinatown like a faded bruise—half massage parlor, half gambling den, half rumor. Neon lights flickered above the narrow doorway, and a single red lantern swayed in the wind, creaking like a warning.

Inside, the place smelled of incense, old cigarettes, and secrets.

But tonight, it was quiet.

Too quiet.

Inside the FBI van, Agents **Knight** and **Barber** zoomed in on the triangulated signal from DJ King's burner call. The last ping landed right in front of The Parlor.

Knight's heart hammered. "This is it. LJ's gotta be inside."

Barber grabbed his gear. "We catch him before DJ shows up, we end this war before it starts."

Knight killed the engine. "Let's move."

They stepped out into the damp night, weapons holstered but ready, eyes scanning the dim alleyways.

The door to The Parlor creaked open.

A woman stumbled out.

Ling Ling.

Her makeup was smeared, hair tangled, blouse ripped at the shoulder like someone had grabbed her too hard. She staggered toward the agents, sobbing, tripping over her own feet.

"Help!" she cried. "Please—please help me!"

Barber rushed forward. "Ma'am, are you hurt? Are you—"

Ling Ling collapsed to her knees, grabbing Barber's pant leg.

"They're inside," she gasped. "They're killing… they're killing everyone. Please—don't let them hurt me—"

Knight scanned the windows. No movement.

"Barber, stay sharp. Something's off."

Ling Ling suddenly looked up at Knight—

And the tears in her eyes stopped.

Just stopped.

Her face shifted from terror to precision, like a mask sliding off.

Knight's stomach dropped.

"BAR—"

He never finished.

Ling Ling's hand snapped behind her back and came

forward holding a **folded micro-chopper**, compact enough to hide in a purse, deadly enough to clear a room.

BRRRRRRRRRRRT—

The muzzle flash lit the parking lot like lightning.

Barber took the full burst to the chest, lifted off his feet, and slammed onto the pavement, blood splattering the van door.

Knight dove for cover, drawing his weapon, but Ling Ling was already airborne—
Leaping sideways behind a parked sedan, landing smooth as a panther.

Knight fired. "FEDERAL AGENT—DROP THE—"

Ling Ling popped up and let the chopper sing again.

BRRRRT—BRRRRT—

Rounds punched into Knight's vest, cracking ribs, spinning him sideways. He gasped, choking on the sudden taste of copper.

He crawled behind a pillar, trying to breathe, trying to steady his gun—

Click.

She was already beside him.

Knight looked up into Ling Ling's face, inches from his.

She wasn't angry.

She wasn't excited.

She was bored.

"Wrong place," she whispered. "Wrong night."

She put the chopper to his throat and pulled the trigger.

His body went slack.

Blood sprayed in an arc across the concrete.

Ling Ling stood, wiped a streak of red from her cheek with the back of her hand, and rolled her neck casually.

The alley was silent again.

She walked over to the FBI van, stepped over Barber's corpse, and opened the driver's door.

Inside, the dashboard glowed with active surveillance tabs—DJ King's tracking files, case notes, LJ's photo pinned on the digital board.

Ling Ling smirked.

"Thank you, boys."

She slid behind the wheel, closed the door, and drove off into the night—

Taking the FBI's entire investigation straight into the hands of the people who were about to tear Houston apart.

The Parlor's red lantern swayed in the breeze, creaking softly, as two federal agents lay dead in the street.

Ling Ling had sprung the trap flawlessly.

And the war had just lost its referees.

CHAPTER 20 – DJ, MAC, AND THE NEPHEW

Harvey Eisenstein's suburban mansion sat quiet under the morning haze, the kind of silence that felt purposeful—like the walls themselves were holding their breath.

DJ King stepped out of the SUV with **Mac** behind him, both men dressed in black, both moving with the kind of confidence that said they have never come to a house uninvited—they arrive owned.

DJ's private maid, **Gloria**, stood at the door already, keys in hand, eyes lowered. DJ had placed her here years ago, a sleeper piece on a chessboard Harvey didn't even know was being played.

"Anyone else home?" DJ asked.

"No, sir," Gloria whispered. "They left early. The wife and the boy… they're upstairs."

DJ nodded. "Good girl. You didn't see us."

She stepped aside silently.

Mac cracked his neck. "You sure LJ's here?"

DJ shot him a look. "I know my blood."

They moved through the immaculate living room—glass sculptures, overpriced art, carpets that had never seen shoes—and then ascended the stairs with the quiet of professional killers.

Halfway up, they heard it.

A rhythmic thud.
A soft moan.
A bed creaking.

Mac raised a brow. "Oh, he definitely here."

DJ didn't smile, but a flicker of amusement touched his eyes.

They reached the hallway.

A door stood cracked open.

Inside, **Michelle** straddled LJ, her hair wild, her body moving like a woman who believed she owned her moment. LJ lay beneath her—naked, quiet, eyes half-lidded but not with pleasure.

He wasn't lost in it.

He was thinking.

Calculating.

The second LJ heard footsteps on the hardwood, something in him **clicked**.

A realization.
A threat.
A choice.

Michelle didn't notice.

"Baby—" she whispered, leaning down to kiss him.

LJ's hand shot to the pillow beside him.

In one fluid motion, he shoved the pillow against Michelle's torso, pressed the barrel of a pistol beneath it—

PFFT—PFFT

Two silenced shots punched through the pillow, through her chest, through her heart.

Michelle spasmed, eyes going wide, shock blooming across her face. For a second, she didn't understand—not that it mattered.

She collapsed forward onto LJ, blood spreading across the sheets.

LJ shoved her off him, breathing hard, face ice-cold.

DJ and Mac stepped into the doorway just as LJ stood and began dressing, calm as a priest putting on Sunday robes.

Mac let out a low whistle. "God damn."

DJ nodded once—pride tempered with grim acceptance. "He's a King."

LJ fastened his watch, grabbed the cash-filled backpack near the nightstand, and finally looked at them.

"Unc," he said, voice steady. "She knew too much."

DJ walked forward, surveyed the body, and didn't even blink. "Michelle always talked too much. She would've given you up eventually."

LJ exhaled, tension leaving his shoulders. "I figured."

"And you acted," DJ said. "That's what matters."

Mac grinned. "Bro, you popped her mid-stroke.

That's some movie shit."

LJ didn't smile. "Can we go?"

DJ placed a hand on LJ's shoulder—heavy, certain, fatherly in a way Lue never was.

"Yeah," DJ said. "Let's get you home."

They descended the stairs together—DJ leading, Mac behind, LJ in the middle.

Three Kings.

A bloodline.

A united front walking straight into a future none of them understood.

Outside, Mac opened the SUV door. LJ climbed in. DJ paused for a moment on the driveway, looking back at the house.

Michelle was dead.
Harvey would soon find out.
And wheels that could never be stopped were officially in motion.

Mac shut the door.

DJ took his seat beside LJ.

As the SUV pulled away, the camera of a security light clicked quietly behind them—sending its footage straight to the one man DJ still trusted.

Lue.

Who watched the feed silently.

Smiled.

And whispered:

"Good, boy."

DJ believed he had reclaimed his nephew—

Not knowing he was walking him deeper into a trap crafted by the two men he least suspected:

Lue King and Harvey Eisenstein.

The Kings rode off together.

United.

Blind.

And officially at war with ghosts they didn't yet see.

CHAPTER 21 – THE FLORES CARTEL FALLS

Club Split's VIP lounge was closed to the public for the night, leaving only a soft blue glow from the bar lights and the rumble of bass leaking through the floorboards. Jasmine King sat at her private booth swirling a drink the color of gold and punishment.

James slid in across from her, dropping a folder thick with intel on the table.

"You hear the news?" he asked, pushing his glasses up.

"I hear everything," Jasmine replied, lifting her glass.

James leaned forward, lowering his voice even though the lounge was empty. "Javier's people just went dark. Completely. Phones dead. Safehouses empty. No bodies yet, but the rumors are loud."

Jasmine took a sip, unbothered.

Then she said it casually, like commenting on the weather.

"Javier's gone."

James blinked. "Gone how?"

She tapped the rim of her glass. "Roxy and her girls."

James froze, processing. "You… you sent Roxy?"

Jasmine nodded.

"But we only agreed to take out Javier," James said slowly. "The plan was to destabilize, not ignite a damn vacuum."

"Oh," Jasmine said lightly, "Juan was there too."

James stared. "Wait—Juan?"

"Yep."

"You killed *both* Flores heirs?"

Jasmine shrugged, swirling her drink again. "Shit happens."

James opened his mouth, closed it, then opened it again. "Jas... you erased their entire leadership in one night."

"And?" Jasmine asked.

"That's not destabilizing—that's annihilation."

A slow smile curled across her lips.

"Exactly."

James sat back, half impressed, half horrified. "Dad's gonna think DJ did it."

"That's the beauty of it," Jasmine said. "The world already blames DJ for Benny. Turk. And now the Flores. Every hit strengthens our position while weakening his. The city feels like it's collapsing under his temper."

"That's... actually brilliant," James admitted.

"I know," she said, taking another sip.

He couldn't argue.

He didn't even want to.

Because the folder he brought wasn't about deaths.

It was about profits.

James slid it toward her. "Look."

Inside were reports from Miami and Vegas:

- **First shipment of Cream: sold out in 48 hours**
- **Nightclubs competing to stock it**
- **Whispers of 'angels' on it, no crash**
- **VIPs paying triple street price**
- **Demand exceeding supply by 300%**

Jasmine's eyes sharpened, the predator behind her calm emerging.

"This is good," she said. "Really good."

James nodded. "Uncle Wesley wants to send two more hearses out this week. Miami wants exclusive rights. Vegas wants bulk shipments. Even LA called."

"LA?" Jasmine asked.

James grinned. "They heard Cream hits different."

Jasmine set her drink down.

"This is it, James. This is our moment. Every cartel boss in the city is panicking. Their networks are fractured. Their leadership is dead or dying. And while they're fighting for scraps…"

She lifted the folder gently, like it was a newborn she was about to raise into a monster.

"...Cream is spreading like gospel."

James exhaled, excitement buzzing through him. "We're about to own the entire nightlife economy."

"No," Jasmine corrected softly. "We're about to own the entire city."

They clinked glasses.

Celebrating the fall of the Flores cartel—

And the rise of something far more dangerous:

the King twins' empire.

Outside, Club Split pulsed harder, brighter, louder.

Almost like the city could feel the shift happening beneath its feet.

The old world was dying.

Cream was the future.

And the Kings were ready to collect every piece.

CHAPTER 22 – THE EMPIRE SHIFTS

The VIP lounge at Club Split felt different tonight.

Not louder. Not busier.

Sharper.

Like the air itself knew plans were being made that could split Houston down its spine.

Jasmine sat at the head of the private table, one leg crossed over the other, a cigarette burning elegantly between her fingers. James spread paperwork and maps across the glass surface—club locations, supply routes, cash projections, and the pieces of the underworld that were slowly, quietly drifting into King hands.

James tapped a map of Houston's nightlife district. "Between Jung's properties and our own clubs, we're sitting on the strongest footprint in the city. Sixty percent of high-traffic nightlife. Seventy if we flip the Westheimer corridor."

Jasmine nodded. "Those numbers give us leverage."

"Against who?" James asked. "The Italians? They've lost half their lieutenants. The rest are broke or scared. They're calling for peace, but they're bleeding."

Jasmine exhaled a long stream of smoke. "Do we

even need the Italians anymore?"

James blinked. "Dad swore loyalty with them twenty years ago."

"And Dad is stuck fighting old wars," Jasmine replied. "We're not."

She picked up a glass marker and circled the Italian-owned clubs on the map with lazy precision.

"They've been relying on our foot traffic for years. Their edges are soft. Their books are cooked. Their security is a joke." She smirked. "Cream could make or break them."

James nodded slowly. "So what's the move? Offer them a cut?"

"Offer some of them a cut," Jasmine corrected. "The ones who know how to stay in line. The others?"

She tapped ash into an empty glass.

"Burn them."

James chuckled. "You know, before tonight I would've questioned that. But after the Flores thing…"

Jasmine tossed him a sideways glance. "Shit happens."

He laughed, shaking his head. "You're terrifying."

"I know," she said without apology.

James leaned over the Vegas and Miami reports. "Cartel influence is shifting too. They're still reeling from Turk's fall and Javier's… disappearance. Miami wants exclusivity. Vegas wants higher volume. The Haitians want to renegotiate terms."

"Give Miami a sweeter deal," Jasmine said. "They spread the fastest."

"And Vegas?"

"Make them beg."

James raised a brow. "And the Haitians?"

Jasmine smiled slowly. "Haitians think they're sharks. But sharks don't survive in shallow water. Raise their price. If they push back, blame supply chain issues."

James scribbled notes. "We really are building our own kingdom."

"No," Jasmine corrected softly. "We're building *the* kingdom."

He paused. "And Dad?"

Jasmine leaned back, eyes glinting.

"Dad is fighting ghosts. He's focused on the big families collapsing. He's focused on LJ. He's focused on war."

James nodded. "Which means he's not watching us."

"Exactly."

She reached for a folder labeled **ITALIAN FAVOR: PENDING**.

James frowned. "You're calling in that one?"

"Maybe," Jasmine said, brushing her thumb along the edge. "The Italians owe us for helping them clean up after the Lucio hit. And I'm thinking we use that favor soon."

James hesitated. "That favor was meant for emergencies."

"This *is* an emergency," Jasmine said. "We're about to reshape the entire playing field. Sometimes you need a quiet knife to finish the cut."

James looked at her, admiration mixed with fear.

"And Dad will never know?" he asked.

Jasmine gave the slightest nod.

"We move clean," she said. "We move smart. And we move without noise."

She stood, smoothing her dress, and tapped the map with her nail.

"We don't need Dad's empire."

James stared at his sister—beautiful, poised, terrifying.

"We're building our own."

The bass from the club below vibrated the floor like a heartbeat.

A new empire forming.

Quiet.
Calculated.
And inevitable.

CHAPTER 23 – HARVEY WALKS IN

Club Split was in full bloom tonight—lines around the block, VIP tables overflowing, dancers threading through the noise like silk. But upstairs, away from the neon and bass, Jasmine and James worked in the quiet hum of their private office.

James adjusted the Miami invoices. Jasmine reviewed projected Cream numbers. They were mid-conversation about expanding to Denver when the knock came.

Three soft taps.
A pause.
Two more.

Jasmine looked up. "That's not security."

James frowned. "Who the hell—? Come in."

The door opened.

Harvey Eisenstein stepped inside.

Perfect suit.
Silver tie clip.
Smile carved from calm arrogance.

The same man whose wife LJ had killed just hours earlier—though the twins didn't know that yet.

Harvey closed the door gently behind him, as if entering a boardroom instead of a den of predators.

"Evening, kids," he said warmly. "Mind if we talk?"

James's stomach tightened.

Jasmine didn't move. Didn't blink. "We didn't schedule anything, Harvey."

Harvey chuckled softly. "Some conversations can't be scheduled."

He stepped fully into the room, hands clasped behind his back like a professor about to give a lecture.

James leaned forward. "Is something wrong?"

"Oh, plenty," Harvey said. "The Flores cartel has collapsed overnight. Javier's missing. Juan too. The Italians are panicking. The city's about to chew its own tongue off."

He smiled wider.

"But none of that's why I'm here."

Jasmine's gaze hardened. "Then why?"

Harvey's eyes flicked briefly—so briefly James almost missed it—to the Cream vials cooling in the mini-fridge beside the bar.

Then to James himself.

"I know you're the creator," Harvey said pleasantly.

James froze.

Jasmine's expression didn't shift, but her fingers curled slightly on the armrest.

Harvey walked past them, tracing a fingertip along

the edge of her desk, admiring the grain.

"Relax," he said softly. "If I wanted to expose you, I wouldn't be standing here. I'm here because... opportunity is loud, and you two? You're the only ones actually listening."

James swallowed. "And what opportunity is that?"

Harvey lowered himself into the chair opposite them.

The smile vanished.

"I know what you're building," he said. "Club networks. Distribution channels. Out-of-state plays. Cream has the potential to swallow the entire southern seaboard. And you two... oh, you children have no idea how big this could get."

Jasmine's eyes narrowed. "What exactly do you want, Harvey?"

He leaned back, crossing his legs, comfortable in the den of lions.

"I want what you want," he said softly. "A new empire."

James and Jasmine exchanged a quick glance—this man was dangerous in ways they hadn't prepared for.

Harvey steepled his fingers.

"And I think," he continued, "we should build it together."

The room fell silent.

The hum of the club below almost felt like the city holding its breath.

Jasmine leaned forward slowly, voice low and lethal.

"And why," she asked, "would *we* partner with you?"

Harvey's smile returned—genuine now, chillingly so.

"Because," he said, "I know where LJ is. I know exactly what happened to the money. And I know who's been pulling the strings behind every murder this week."

James tensed.

Jasmine's pulse flickered in her jaw.

Harvey folded his hands, eyes bright.

"And I think it's time," he whispered, "that the three of us stop reacting…
and start ruling."

He waited.

Smiling.

Knowing he had just dropped the kind of truth no one could ignore.

Knowing this conversation—this moment—would change everything.

The chapter ends there.

A cliffhanger.

Harvey, smiling politely.

Jasmine and James, calculating.

And the entire King empire about to pivot toward something far more dangerous than war—

ambition.

—

will become the battleground for a war none of them are ready for.

The empire is shifting.
The wolves are circling.
And the Kings are running out of time.

CHAPTER 24 – HARVEY'S COLLAPSE

The Eisenstein house was too quiet.

DJ King stepped out of the SUV with Mac flanking him, both moving fast and low. No security. No dogs. No lights except the dim glow spilling through Harvey's office window.

A bad sign.

A very bad sign.

Mac checked the perimeter with a quick sweep of his rifle. "House feels dead, Unc."

DJ's jaw tightened. "Then Harvey's hiding something."

They crossed the lawn, boots brushing through the manicured grass, and approached the side door. It was unlocked—another warning.

DJ didn't hesitate.

He pushed it open.

Inside, the house looked staged for a magazine: perfectly arranged pillows, spotless marble, a grand piano that hadn't been touched in years. But the silence in the air was wrong—too heavy, too expectant, like the house was holding its breath.

Mac whispered, "Why we here again?"

DJ didn't look back. "Because Harvey's been lying. And liars get sloppy."

They rounded the corner into the hall leading to Harvey's home office. DJ stopped.

The door was cracked open.
Light spilled from inside.
Someone was pacing.

DJ raised a fist.

Mac froze in place.

DJ pushed the door open with two fingers.

Harvey Eisenstein stood at his desk, breathing hard, shirt untucked, hands shaking as he trafficked papers into a suitcase. The phone on the desk buzzed nonstop, a stream of missed calls filling the screen:

LUE KING (4 missed calls)
UNKNOWN (2)
REDLINE HOLDINGS (3)

Harvey didn't notice DJ at first.

He just whispered to himself:

"He killed Michelle… he killed Michelle… I need to get out. I need to get out before—"

DJ stepped inside.

"Before what?" he asked.

Harvey spun around, pale as bone, fear flooding his face.

"D-DJ—Jesus—you scared me—"

"Why'd you run?" DJ asked, voice soft but lethal.

Harvey swallowed. "Run? I wasn't—DJ, listen, we can talk—"

Mac stepped in behind DJ. "Harvey. Stop lying."

Harvey's eyes darted to the suitcase, then to DJ.

"Your... your nephew killed my wife," Harvey said, voice cracking. "I didn't know where else to go. I panicked."

DJ nodded slowly. "So you were leaving town."

"I just—I needed time to think—"

"You were leaving," DJ repeated.

Harvey's breathing sped up. He took a small step backward. "DJ, please. I raised LJ like my own. I protected him. I protected *you*. I've always been loyal."

DJ walked toward him.

A slow, steady, terrifying walk.

"Loyalty," DJ said softly, "isn't something you say, Harv."

He stopped a foot away.

"It's something you *prove*."

Harvey's voice dropped to a whisper. "DJ... I didn't steal the money."

DJ's expression never changed. "That's not why I'm here."

Harvey blinked. "Then—then what—?"

DJ glanced at the buzzing phone. "I want to know what you and my brother been whispering about."

Harvey's face collapsed.

And that one flinch told DJ everything he needed to know.

"DJ—please—just listen—"

But DJ had already made his decision.

He stepped forward, wrapped one hand around the back of Harvey's neck, and lowered his forehead until it pressed against Harvey's.

Harvey trembled. "DJ—don't—please—your family is being used—you don't understand—"

"I understand enough," DJ whispered.

He drew the pistol from his coat.

Harvey's knees buckled. "DJ—DJ, WAIT—IT WASN'T ME—IT WAS—"

THUD.

DJ fired once into Harvey's chest.

Harvey crashed backward onto the hardwood, gasping, eyes wide with shock and betrayal.

Mac winced. "Damn."

Harvey clawed weakly at DJ's pant leg. "Lue… Lue… did this… not me…"

DJ stared down at him, face unreadable.

Harvey's voice rasped, broken, desperate:
"He's... using your nephew... he's... using your... your whole... family..."

His hand fell flat.

His breath stopped.

Harvey Eisenstein was dead.

The one man who could have proven Lue's betrayal was gone forever.

DJ holstered the gun, exhaling slowly. "Clean it up."

Mac nodded, stepping into the room to wipe down surfaces, close blinds, and prepare the scene.

DJ turned to leave, but paused at the doorway and whispered:

"Should've stayed loyal, Harv."

He walked out into the night.

Behind him, Harvey's phone buzzed one last time:

LUE KING – Incoming Call

Mac silenced it with his boot.

The King empire had just lost one of its architects—and DJ didn't even know he'd shot the wrong man.

The collapse had begun.

CHAPTER 25 – JAMES SEES THE CRACKS

The King estate slept under a velvet-black sky.

Jasmine had left hours earlier for a late meeting at Club Split. DJ and Mac were still out—handling business James wasn't invited to. The house felt too big, too cold, too full of shadows that didn't belong to him.

James wandered the upstairs hallway barefoot, glasses pushed up in his hair, mind racing with numbers—Cream projections, club turnover, Miami expansion—trying to calm himself with math the way other people used religion.

He stopped outside his father's old study.

A faint light glowed underneath the door.

Lue King shouldn't have been home.
He was supposed to be at a meeting in Bellaire.

James tilted his head, listening.

Voices.

Low. Urgent.

He moved closer.
Pressed his ear to the doorframe.

He didn't mean to eavesdrop.

But once he heard the first sentence, he couldn't

move.

"...Harvey is down. DJ took him out faster than I expected."

Lue's voice.

Smooth. Cold. Calculating.

James's blood froze.

Another voice responded—older, accented, someone he didn't recognize.

"Does this change your timeline?"

"No," Lue said. "Harvey out of the picture complicates distribution, but it also blinds DJ. He'll take the bait harder now."

James swallowed, heartbeat thudding in his ears.

The stranger spoke again. "And the boy? LJ?"

"He's tucked away. Useful. The city believes he stole the money. DJ believes he's innocent. Both positions benefit me."

James covered his mouth.

His father...

His *father*...

Was talking about LJ like he was a pawn.

Like he wasn't family.

Lue continued:

"DJ's too sentimental. Can't see the bigger picture. He's reacting—killing everything in front of him.

Exactly the chaos we need."

The stranger chuckled. "And the twins?"

James stiffened.

Lue exhaled.

"Jasmine is predictable. Ambitious. Ruthless. She'll take more territory without hesitation. She clears the board for me."

James's stomach dropped.

"And James?" the man asked.

Lue paused.

Too long.

"James is brilliant," Lue said finally. "But he's soft. He thinks blood means loyalty. He'll break soon… and when he does, he'll choose me."

The stranger hummed. "Because he fears DJ?"

"No," Lue replied quietly. "Because he needs to be special. And DJ will never make him feel that way."

James's hand trembled against the doorframe.

He remembered being eight years old—DJ teaching him how to shoot.
He remembered being twelve—DJ putting an arm around him when Lue forgot his birthday.
He remembered being seventeen—DJ calling him "the future of this family."

Special.

DJ always treated him like he mattered.

Lue…

Lue apparently saw him as a tool.

James's throat tightened.

Inside, the conversation continued:

"Once DJ is isolated," Lue said, "Harvey gone, the Italians softened, the Flores erased… the city will be ready. Book Two is the takeover."

"Ambitious," the stranger said.

"Necessary," Lue answered. "DJ's time is ending. The new empire begins with me. And my children will stand beside me—or fall under me."

James staggered backward, breath shaking.

His father wasn't just planning a takeover.

He was planning a **coup**.

A betrayal.

A war against DJ.

Against the entire family.

Footsteps shifted inside the room.

Chairs scraped.

James panicked and moved away—quiet, fast—slipping down the hallway and ducking into a guest room just as the door opened behind him.

He held his breath.

Lue's voice drifted into the hallway.

"Make sure everything is ready. We move soon."

Footsteps faded.

James stayed frozen until the house fell silent.

Then he collapsed onto the bed, burying his face in his hands.

His father...
The one he idolized...
The man he spent his whole life trying to impress...

Was the enemy.

Cracks spiderwebbed through James's chest—between the family he loved, the empire he wanted to build, and the truth he could no longer unhear.

He wiped his eyes, breathing hard.

For the first time in his life, James King felt something break deep inside him.

Something he wasn't sure he'd ever get back.

CHAPTER 26 – LOYALTY & LIES

James barely slept.

The fragments of his father's conversation replayed in endless loops:

"...Harvey is down. DJ took him out faster than I expected."
"...LJ is tucked away. Useful."
"...James is brilliant, but he's soft. He'll choose me eventually."
"...My children will stand beside me—or fall under me."

By dawn, James felt hollow.

He dressed slowly—black hoodie, jeans, glasses smudged from rubbing tired eyes—then walked downstairs toward DJ's study.

He stopped halfway down the stairs.

DJ was already awake, standing in the foyer, coat on, talking quietly with two of his lieutenants. His face was harder than usual, as if whatever he'd done last night had taken a piece out of him.

When DJ noticed James, he waved the others away and waited until they were alone.

"You okay, son?" DJ asked.

James swallowed.

DJ rarely called him *son*.
That word made his throat tighten.

James nodded weakly. "Yeah. Just… long night."

DJ stepped closer, studying him.

"You look like hell."

James cracked a humorless smile. "Thanks."

DJ's tone softened. "What's going on?"

James opened his mouth.

He wanted to tell the truth.

He wanted to say *Dad is plotting against you.*
He wanted to say *Lue stole the money.*
He wanted to say *LJ is being used like bait.*
He wanted to say *I'm scared.*

But the words didn't come.

He couldn't betray Lue—not yet.
He couldn't betray DJ by staying silent—yet he did.

James looked down at the floor. "Just… pressure from the club expansion. Cream distribution. Been working nonstop."

DJ nodded slowly, placing a hand on James's shoulder.

"You're carrying more than you should," DJ said. "But you're doing damn good. Better than I ever did at your age."

James blinked hard, eyes burning.

DJ squeezed his shoulder gently. "You're a leader,

James. Houston's gonna follow you one day. Don't forget that."

James looked up.

DJ meant it.

DJ *believed* in him.

And that made the silence feel like betrayal sliding down his throat.

"Unc…" James said quietly. "If I ever… if I ever hear something off… something dangerous… you'd want me to come to you, right?"

DJ didn't hesitate. "Always. Family protects family."

James nodded slowly.

Lying by omission.

Bleeding on the inside.

DJ stepped back. "Listen—I gotta make moves today. Big ones. You and Jasmine keep handling the expansion. We're almost through the storm."

James didn't respond.

Because he knew the truth:

The storm was just beginning.

DJ turned and walked out the door, leaving the house with purpose in his stride.

James stood frozen in the quiet foyer, tears threatening but refusing to fall.

He whispered to himself:

"I'm sorry."

Sorry for staying silent.
Sorry for choosing loyalty to the wrong man.
Sorry for being exactly what Lue called him—

Soft.

But under that apology, something else formed.

A shadow.

A new silence.

A slow shift in loyalty he didn't fully understand yet.

James wiped his face.

Then he whispered:

"…Dad will explain everything."

But James didn't believe it.

Not really.

He walked upstairs, sat on the edge of his bed, and buried his face in his hands.

Silence was a choice.

And he had just made the worst one of his life.

CHAPTER 27 – A KING'S SON

James didn't go to Club Split.

He didn't check inventory, didn't call Jasmine, didn't handle shipments or returns or the ten other tasks he usually crushed without blinking.

He sat in his room.

Lights off. Curtains closed.

His laptop glowed faintly on the desk, spreadsheets waiting, projections unfinished. Numbers had always been his sanctuary—but today, even the math felt wrong.

The house creaked.

A soft knock tapped on his door.

James didn't answer.

The door opened anyway.

Lue King stepped inside wearing a cardigan, slacks, and slippers—dressed like a man who'd never fired a weapon, never stolen a billion dollars, never orchestrated a citywide collapse.

"Son," Lue said gently. "We need to talk."

James stiffened on the edge of the bed but didn't look up.

Lue closed the door behind him. "I heard you didn't leave your room today."

James stayed silent.

Lue crossed the room and sat beside him, not too close—just close enough.

"You look like your mother when you're troubled," Lue said softly. "She'd go quiet. Retreat inside herself. You got that from her."

James's chest tightened.

He hated when Lue used his mother like a tool.

"Hear me out," Lue continued. "I can feel something's wrong. And I want to help."

James bit the inside of his cheek.

His father's voice, calm and steady, made it harder to breathe.

Lue folded his hands. "Is this about DJ?"

James's eyes flickered.

Barely noticeable.

But Lue caught it.

He exhaled, a fatherly sigh he had practiced for years. "You don't have to pretend, James. I know things are... unstable."

James looked at him for the first time.

"Unstable?" James whispered. "You mean the bodies stacked every night? The money missing? The city on fire? Or the fact that DJ is walking around killing the wrong people?"

Lue didn't flinch.

If anything, he looked... proud.

"You're seeing clearly," Lue said. "Not emotionally. Logically. Rationally. That's why you're different from DJ."

James swallowed. "You two used to be close."

Lue chuckled sadly. "Until he decided blood only matters when he says it does."

James frowned. "What does that mean?"

Lue looked him in the eye.

Really looked.

"Your uncle," Lue said slowly, "loves you. But he'll never see you as a leader. Not truly. He sees Jasmine. He sees LJ. He sees Mac. But you—James—you've outgrown the little box he put you in."

James felt his throat tighten.

"He does see me," James said, but the words sounded weak even to his own ears.

Lue's voice dropped to a whisper. "Does he?"

James didn't answer.

Because deep down—buried under years of polite smiles and leadership lessons and backhanded compliments—he had always wondered if DJ saw him the way he saw Jasmine:

Strong. Unbreakable. Capable of running an empire.

Lue placed a hand on James's shoulder.

"You're the smartest one in this family," Lue said.

"And DJ knows it. That's why he keeps you close—but never lets you lead."

James closed his eyes.

It hurt because it wasn't entirely wrong.

"I want you to have what you deserve," Lue said. "Not scraps. Not permission. Not whatever role DJ decides to hand out when he's done tearing Houston apart."

James whispered, "What role do *you* think I deserve?"

Lue smiled—soft, fatherly, calculated.

"Your own throne."

Those three words slipped into James like a drug.

A slow, warm poison.

Lue leaned closer. "You're my son. A King. The empire is your birthright—not something you wait for someone else to give you."

James's breath trembled.

"But DJ—"

"DJ is blinded by loyalty and sentiment," Lue said. "He'll drag this family into the grave with him. Someone intelligent has to step up."

James felt dizzy.

His father's hand on his shoulder.

His uncle's words from earlier: *You're a leader, James.*

Two different visions of him.

Two different futures.

One burning question:

Who should he believe?

Lue lowered his voice even more. "I know you overheard something last night."

James's heart stopped.

Lue continued, calm as ever. "I saw your reflection in the glass. I knew you were there."

James's stomach twisted.

"But I didn't stop," Lue said gently. "Because I trust you. I trust that you'll understand what I'm trying to build. I trust that you'll see DJ isn't thinking about your future… but I am."

James covered his mouth with his hand.

He wasn't just caught.

He was being *embraced.*

Manipulated.

Guided.

Loved the wrong way.

Lue rose to his feet and kissed the top of James's head —something he hadn't done in years.

"You're my son," Lue whispered. "And we're going to change this city together."

He walked toward the door.

Paused.

Turned back.

"And James?"

James looked up, eyes glassy.

"When the time comes," Lue said, "you'll need to choose a side. Choose the one that sees who you truly are."

The door closed.

Silence swallowed the room.

James put his head in his hands and sobbed—quiet, broken, not from fear...

...but from knowing Lue was right about one thing:

He *had* been waiting for DJ to see him.

And now someone else had.

Even if it was the devil.

CHAPTER 28 – BEFORE THE FALL

Houston didn't sleep that night.

Not really.

The city buzzed with sirens, unmarked vans, late-night news choppers, and the restless hum of an underworld that felt the ground shifting beneath it.

DJ King stood alone on the balcony of his estate, the wind brushing across his face as dawn crept over the skyline. He'd changed into a fresh suit, poured a glass of cognac, and lit a cigar—but none of it settled the tight coil in his chest.

Too much death.
Too many questions.
Too much silence where there should've been answers.

Behind him, the sliding glass door opened.

Mac stepped out, moving quietly.

"They're sayin' the Feds found the van," Mac said. "Or... what's left of it."

DJ exhaled through his nose. "Knight and Barber?"

"Dead."

DJ didn't look surprised.

Ling Ling's name hadn't been said, but they both

knew.

"The Bureau thinks it's connected to us," Mac continued. "They're tightening up across the city. They want LJ bad."

DJ nodded once. "It was bound to happen."

Mac leaned on the balcony rail, eyes scanning the estate. "We need to pull back. Lay low."

"No," DJ said, voice steady. "We move forward. Fast."

Mac frowned. "We just hit Turk. Took out half the city leadership. Javier's gone. Jung's son's missing fingers. We might be movin' too fast."

DJ took a slow pull from his cigar.

"We're not moving fast enough."

Mac stared at him, then sighed. "Unc... you ain't been right since earlier."

DJ's jaw flexed.

"I handled something wrong," he said quietly. "I can feel it."

Mac waited.

DJ didn't elaborate.

Couldn't.

Not yet.

A door opened downstairs. Footsteps approached. Jasmine's voice—sharp, irritated—drifted up.

"Dad!"

Only Jasmine used that tone on him.

DJ turned as she stepped onto the balcony, heels clacking, black dress from the night before still flawless. James followed behind her, expression pale, distant.

"We need to talk," Jasmine said.

DJ raised an eyebrow. "About?"

"Cream," Jasmine replied. "We can't keep moving like this without more manpower. Miami wants double the shipment next week. Vegas too. And now people are asking questions about Harvey."

DJ stared at her.

"You worried about Cream," he said flatly, "after the week we just had?"

Jasmine crossed her arms. "Cream is our future. If you want us to run this empire, we need prep, security, bodies, infrastructure. We can't just improvise every night."

DJ turned to James. "You agree?"

James shifted, hands in pockets. His eyes avoided DJ's.

"I… think Jas has a point," he said quietly.

DJ narrowed his eyes.

Something was off with James. Something dark and new.

"We'll address it," DJ said. "But first we have bigger

problems."

Jasmine folded her arms. "Bigger than Cream?"

"Bigger than all of it," DJ said. "We got set up. Someone used LJ. Someone stole the money. Someone hit every family in one night—including ours."

Jasmine's shrug covered a flicker of fear. James looked down at the floor.

Mac stepped forward. "Unc thinks there's a traitor in the city."

DJ corrected him.

"In the family."

Silence dropped heavy as concrete.

James's stomach flipped. Jasmine stiffened.

"Who?" she whispered.

DJ didn't answer.

Because he didn't know.

Not yet.

But his instincts were screaming.

Something was wrong.
Something under the surface.
Something moving in the dark where bloodlines twisted and loyalties blurred.

Before DJ could explain further, the front gate buzzed—relentless, loud, echoing through the house.

Mac checked his phone, eyes widening.

"Unc… it's the FBI."

Jasmine cursed under her breath. "Shit—already?"

James looked sick.

DJ stubbed out his cigar and stood.

"Stay inside," he ordered.

"Dad—" Jasmine started.

"Inside," DJ repeated, voice like steel.

Mac followed him toward the stairs. "You want me on the back side?"

DJ shook his head. "We're not running."

"But they're—"

"We're not running," DJ said again. "Let them in. Let them talk. Let them think they're getting somewhere."

The two men descended.

Jasmine watched them go. James leaned on the railing, hands shaking silently.

She looked at him. "What's wrong with you?"

James didn't answer.

Because he couldn't tell her the truth:

He wasn't afraid of the FBI.
He wasn't afraid of the city.
He wasn't afraid of the bloodshed.

He was afraid of their father.

He was afraid of the truth sitting in his chest like a live grenade.

Jasmine reached for him. "James?"

He flinched away.

"I'm fine," he murmured, voice cracking.

The FBI lights flashed outside, blue and red reflecting across the estate windows like war paint.

Downstairs, DJ opened the door.

The agents stepped forward.

The war drums of Book Two began beating.

Jasmine inhaled sharply, realizing the storm she felt in her bones wasn't just paranoia.

James whispered something she barely heard:

"Dad… is going to destroy this family."

Jasmine froze.

"What did you just say?"

But James didn't repeat it.

He just looked out at the flashing lights, eyes full of fear and destiny.

Inside, DJ faced the agents without blinking.

His final thought before the agents spoke:

Enough is enough.
No more mercy.
No more business as usual.

DJ raised his chin, bracing for the beginning of the

end.

And with the weight of an entire empire on his shoulders, he whispered to himself:

"Everything before today was business."

The agents began reading the warrant.

DJ's hands curled into fists.

"What comes next…" he murmured.

The wind picked up, howling through the open door.

"…is personal."

END OF BOOK ONE

www.ingramcontent.com/pod-product-compliance
Lightning Source LLC
Chambersburg PA
CBHW022036220526
45357CB00059B/288